MONKEY
AND BLAIN

A COLLECTION OF CONVERSATIONS
AND GENERAL NONSENSE

COAUTHORED BY
**MONKEY AND
BLAIN DIEBOLT**

outskirts
press

Monkey and Blain
A Collection of conversations and general nonsense
All Rights Reserved.
Copyright © 2020 CoAuthored by Monkey and Blain Diebolt
v2.0

This is a work of fiction. Names, characters, businesses, places, events, locales, and incidents are either the products of the author's imagination or used in a fictitious manner. Any resemblance to actual persons, living or dead, or actual events is purely coincidental.

The opinions expressed in this manuscript are solely the opinions of the author and do not represent the opinions or thoughts of the publisher. The author has represented and warranted full ownership and/or legal right to publish all the materials in this book.

This book may not be reproduced, transmitted, or stored in whole or in part by any means, including graphic, electronic, or mechanical without the express written consent of the publisher except in the case of brief quotations embodied in critical articles and reviews.

Outskirts Press, Inc.
http://www.outskirtspress.com

Paperback ISBN: 978-1-9772-2342-5

Cover Photo © 2020 www.gettyimages.com.. All rights reserved - used with permission.

Outskirts Press and the "OP" logo are trademarks belonging to Outskirts Press, Inc.

PRINTED IN THE UNITED STATES OF AMERICA

For Yoma, Love Yoson.

BOOK DISCLAIMER

The thoughts and beliefs, words and actions of Monkey and Blain are solely their's and not necessarily the thoughts and beliefs, words or actions of their employer, family, friends, political affiliation, religion, neighbors, acquaintances, Facebook friends, government, coworkers, past or present, or anyone else you can think of, and are not on behalf of any organization, employee, etc. Any blame, hurt feelings, intolerance perceived (yep everyone wants a trophy), anger, sadness, conviction, or any other buzz word you can think of, should be directed at Blain and Monkey only, and as stated, do not reflect the position of any employer or group of people (we are individuals people). If you have an issue with the words in the book, you probably need a nap... maybe an enema. It will be ok people. Unclench and relax.

FORWARD AND INTRODUCTION OF MONKEY BY BLAIN

My name is Blain, I am both the 10th man and 13th monkey. I believe Monkey was born when I was born. When I was younger, Monkey would do the naughty things, and I was the innocent one. You were either talking to Monkey or me. In September 2012, I volunteered for a month long detail in the Washington DC area for my employment. My employment is already a bit stressful, but being from Iowa and new to the job, I was NOT ready for the DC area. My first day there, all I did was fly in, drive an hour to the hotel and checked in. 10 miles = 1 hour time. It is not an exaggeration, I did not believe it when I was warned ahead of time. So 1st day my stress level is pretty high, 23 days to go. Day 2 I sat in my rented car, nearly in tears because I couldn't figure out where to eat. Nearly in tears. I was on the edge. I think that is where monkey came forward to live in tandem with me. With a nearly audible pop, Monkey was now with me. He didn't start having conversations with me yet, but from day 2 on in DC, Monkey did the stressful things, and I was along for the ride. In November 2012, Monkey addressed me directly. At this time, he was just IIM (Imaginary Invisible Monkey). From December 2012 to today, he is just Monkey. Monkey and I talk regularly.

We all talk to ourselves, it is just a fact. I know I am not insane, I've just named my other half of the conversations. I understand that crazy people don't think they are crazy either. Monkey says the things I can't, or shouldn't. Monkey is a bit crass, rude and inappropriate, but he is a good monkey. My filter is around 50%, Monkey's is around 15%. I'm working on my filter, Monkey doesn't care. In this book are actual conversations between Monkey and Me. The range of dates are the end of 2012 to November 2019. Only select conversations have been included. It has been 7 years and not all of them were recorded or remembered.

Why write a book? Well, for years I have been saying that I would. Monkey and my conversations, some but not all, were posted on Facebook for 7 years. I came to the point in my life that if I want to encourage people to follow their dreams and try new things, I should do what I say also. I'm pretty sure I will have to go squatching sometime now too. Another reason for the book is that I read in a book the secret of immortality. It is pretty simple, tell your story. It isn't for me to have immortality, I believe in God, I already have eternal life. It is for Monkey to become immortal. Follow your dreams people, do what you say you have wanted to do. It may be a huge fiery failure, do it anyway. You don't know what you don't know. You wont know if you don't try. Be unafraid to find out what you do or do not like. The original plan is a total of 3 books. Time will tell. The order of the two remaining books will depend on the amount of participation of the reader. The upcoming book 'Ask Monkey Anything' will be where the reader can go to the Facebook page to ask questions that will be answered by Monkey in the book. It will be around 100-150ish questions answered in the book. The other book will be titled "Monkey and Blain...but wait, there's more!' and will be more conversations between Monkey and me. The books are mostly me fulfilling my end by doing what I said I would do, and to share Monkey with the world. If you enjoy it, let Monkey know. Monkey loves this, I'm just along for the ride. Be kind, be just, be honest, and follow your dreams.

List of Thanks: Thank you Father God, for providing all my needs and most of my wants. Thank you family and friends for putting up with me and encouragement while taking this journey. Thank YOU who are reading this. I didn't want to list people individually because i think i would have missed someone and then felt horrible. If you know me, I appreciate you. If you have heard of me, HI. If you found this by accident, enjoy.

God bless you and your families.

Blain Diebolt 11/2019.

FORWARD AND INTRO BY MONKEY

MY TURN! Blain said he would not alter or redact anything I write in the forward, as long as it didn't include swearing. Blain is bat crap crazy. Not in a dangerous or violent way, just in a delusional, voice hearing way. We talk everyday. EVERY DAY! The guy never shuts up. Since we exist at the same time now, Blain is the one you see (mostly), but the words coming out of his mouth are both of ours. I can now, after I ended the Mayan Apocalypse, appear physically, but most of the time I just remain inside Blain's mind and visible to him only. He always sees me, if you are lucky you may too. Peas and carrots.

I'm not a big fan of warning labels, but since people are kinda stupid, I feel the need for one;

I, Monkey, exist only in Blain's head. I am not real. Do NOT do anything that I suggest doing in the book, don't be a jackass. Most are not good ideas. This is your warning. Your actions are your responsibility. Saddle up, enjoy the show.

Bat crap crazy remember. Thanks for reading. If you enjoyed this book, please participate in the future book 'Ask Monkey Anything'. Go to Facebook- **Monkey and Blain**. I promise to be as honest, blunt and direct as possible. Remember that I make stuff up though. Should be a full on Non-PC, offensive, intolerant, laughfest.....or not, don't care. Play! Be unique, follow your dreams, fulfill your word.

Steaksauce.

Monkey 11/2019

Monkey: Blain, we put a warning label at the beginning of the book, right?

Blain: Yep, too many lawsuits. Had to state 'do not do this at home'.

Monkey: What did people do before lawsuits?

Blain: Survived. We didn't wear helmets when riding bikes, watched cartoons that didn't have warnings, where things blew up, ate red meat, eggs and donuts, and we all came out ok.

Monkey: You sure?

Blain: For the most part.

Monkey: Yeah, so what happened?

Blain: I think it started with someone getting their leg burnt by coffee.

Monkey: Cause coffee isn't typically hot.

Blain: Exactly.

Monkey: Touchy feely crap.

Blain: Indeed.

Monkey: I gotta poop....on with the show.

** First actual conversation with Monkey*** 11/6/2012

IIM: Hey Blain?

Blain: yes imaginary invisible monkey?

IIM: Whatchu doing?

Blain: I'm trying to work.

IIM: Wanna go play in the rain?

Blain: No, I can't, I need to get this report done.

IIM: Wanna take a nap?

Blain: Yes I do, but I need to get this report done.

IIM: Wanna fling some poo?

Blain: no, I have to.....well ok, lets go fling some poo.

END OF THE WORLD 2012

IIM: Hey Blain?

Blain: Yes?

IIM: They are gonna stop making Twinkies.

Blain: I heard. Do you know why?

IIM: Cause we elected socialists?

Blain: That's right monkey.

IIM: Hey Blain? This is the beginning of The End, isn't it?

Blain: Yes Monkey, it is. Are you frightened?

IIM: Nope, I'm not real. Are you?

Blain: Nope, I know Jesus. Just waiting on my ticket home.

Thankfully we know that Twinkies came back. God Bless the U.S.A.

monkey makes audio recordings for 2012 end of the world

IIM: The End is coming. THE End, Capital E! Monkey/human hybrids are coming, the sun is burning out, the aliens have landed, the bees have died, the government won, common sense is gone. We poisoned our lands, food, water, air, minds, children, parents, thoughts, actions, intentions, and beliefs. It is time to move to the mountains. Gather your supplies, make a plan, move to the hills. You only have room for 1 backpack per person. Will have to walk, don't take your car, they are being tracked. Don't bring your phones, they are being tracked. No electricity, no running water. Build a house, post a guard, protect your family. Monkey and Blain love you. End of message.

IIM: Ok, Blain stepped out of the office and im here on Facebook. That guy eats like a 4 year old, and farts in his sleep. This is monkey LIVE in Cedar Rapids IA, bringing your countdown to the end of the world. I will be giving you updates throughout these last 14 days. So far, nothing has happened. This has been monkey live from Cedar Rap...

Blain: Hey monkey, what are you doing?

IIM: Public Service Announcements. Maybe you should get back to work.

Blain: Yes boss.

IIM: It's monkey live in Cedar Rapids IA on 12/09/2012....still no zombies, no polar shifts, no sun explosions, no planet X sighting, no vampires, haven't seen Jesus yet, no Mayans, no hindus, no snow....I did however see Bigfoot, he is doing good, but that is not on the schedule for the 12/21/2012 countdown. In short, nothing. This has been monkey reporting from....wait is that a zombie? Oops, nevermind, live from Cedar Rapids IA, monkey live.

IIM: This is monkey reporting live in Cedar Rapids IA, it is 12/12/2012....it would be cooler if the year was actually 12....then it would be 12/12/12.....anyhow, update on The End of the world; today in Iowa City zombies were seen walking in the streets....what?....This just in, they were NOT zombies, they were college students walking in the streets during finals week. Ok, this one is real, something about an asteroid grazing the earth....Again? You have to be kidding me.....This just in, the Asteroid was actually 4.3 Million miles away....not exactly grazing the earth....lastly, in Cedar Rapids IA at approximately 10:15pm, I monkey, saw again, yes again, Bigfoot.....ok, I didn't see bigfoot. This End of the world news sucks, nothing is happening. This has been monkey live in Cedar Rapids IA.

IIM: Monkey here, reporting live in Cedar Rapids IA. There is still nothing going on. It is 12/16/2012, shouldn't there be something going on by now? Anyhow, we successfully traveled to the Quad Cities to check out the scene there. Wanted to see some people too. No zombies, no Mayans, no polar shifts, no solar flares there either. I'm watching a program called 'surviving zombies'....something like that, just in case. To sum up, nothing going on with 5 days left of the world, this has been monkey live.

Blain: You still doing the recordings?

IIM: yep for posterity.....or something.

Blain: And who is it that made you The End commentator?

IIM: You didn't want to do it.

Blain: True.

IIM: Monkey live in Cedar Rapids IA.

Blain: Monkey is a little under the weather and wanted me to record the exact time the world is to end. He googled something and it said the end will happen on 12/21/2012 at 11:11 UTC, which turns out is the same as GMT....so, here in the Midwest that is minus 5 hours, making it 5:11 AM on 12/21/2012...does that sound right monkey?

IIM: Well done human, have a cookie.

Blain: Wiseass.....I WILL take that cookie though.

IIM: Close it out.

Blain: So lame.....Blain live in Cedar Rapids IA.

IMM: Here is your cookie.

IIM: IT'S THE END! IN APPROXIMATELY 8 HOURS WE ARE ALL GONNA DIE! I CAN'T DO THE COUNTDOWN, I'M SO SCARED!!!...

Blain: It's Tuesday.

IIM: What?

Blain: It's only Tuesday. Thursday is the big day.

IIM: Tuesday?

Blain: Yep, you have 2 full days before total freak out.

IIM: That is kinda disappointing....in that case....This is monkey live in Cedar Rapids IA, there are approximately 56 hours left until the zombie/asteroid/solar flare/mayan death curse/earthquake/spontaneous combustion end of the world. As of today, 12/19/2012, there have been zero sightings of zombies, vampires, or snow. If anyone finds these recordings, was there any warning before the actual day for you? It is all work and no play here in Cedar Rapids, Blain is getting kinda tired and cranky. This has been monkey live in Cedar Rapids IA.

Blain: Nice recovery monkey.

IIM: Thanks. Sorry about the freak out. Can I have ice cream?

Blain: I think you have earned it today.

IIM: YAYYYYYYYYYYYYYYYYYYY!

the big day 12/21/2012

IIM: Blain....I feel weird...

Blain: Like sick weird?

IIM: Like weird weird, like heavy.

Blain: AHHHHHHH!

IIM: AHHHHHHH! WHAT?

Blain: You have a shadow!

IIM: What in the.....

Blain: I can see you.

IIM: I can see you too!

Blain: No, I mean you are physically....you have.....

IIM fully enters the physical world

IIM: I HAD to do it Blain. I had to come free from your sight only, to enter into the physical plane. Other's can now see me, if i choose. I did this to save the world.

Blain: You knew this before?

IIM: Nope, it just came to me. You're welcome.

Blain: Do we tell people that you saved the world?

IIM: From now on, I am just 'Monkey'. Share it with the world.

Blain: I will sound like a madman.

Monkey: Then madmen....madmonkeys....mad we will be.

Blain: Works for me. What is the proof that you saved the world?

Monkey: It's still here, right?

Blain: Sounds legit. You had a big day, want some ice cream?

Monkey: ICE CREAM!

Monkey: Holy Crap, I can see the Matrix!

Blain: Don't screw around monkey, not funny.

Monkey: No seriously, it is a lot worse than I thought!

Blain: Really? What is it like?

Monkey: I'm just messing with you.

Blain: Oh good. I'm not sure I could handle if this wasn't the 'real' version if this was supposed to be the 'best' version of reality.

Monkey: Exactly...if this is the best version, there is no hope.

Blain: I'm going to a better place.

Monkey: can I go too?

Blain: Darn tootin.

Monkey: Can we shoot fireworks?

Blain: Sure.

Monkey: Can we ride dinosaurs?

Blain: If they are there.

Monkey: steak sauce!

Blain: Ok monkey, timeout is over.

Monkey: YAYYYYY! Monkey live here in Cedar Rapids IA with your 2013 predictions....First of all 'timeout' was bullcrap. I did NOT throw poop at the neighbor or ride the neighbor's dog like a rodeo bull.

Blain: You did, and you are sorry....right?

Monkey: Ok, I did, and im sorry.....anyhow, 2013 predictions; Number 1 People will still not take responsibility for their actions, blame others for their mistakes and failures, and generally be just as self centered and out for themselves as in the past. Number 2 2013 will be another touchy feely year. We won't use words like 'fail' or 'unacceptable'. Everyone will be ok and no one's feelings will get hurt. Number 3 They 'government' will always be after your guns, get used to it, get used to paying more for less of things too. Number 4 there will be wars and rumors of wars, cause the End is near. Number 5 * BLEEP BLEEP BLEEP BLEEP BLEEP*!

Blain: MONKEY! No Swearing!

Monkey: Oops. Sorry....Number 6 the winning powerball numbers are 6, 7, 9, 19, 32, and the powerball is 13....date of drawing not included. Number 7 Blain will keep snoring and farting in his sleep. Number 8 I will probably still throw poop and generally get into trouble on the regular you. Number 9 US's credit rating will drop again. Lastly, Number 10 day will be light, night will be dark, summer is hot and winter is cold, but with all that happening, remember that Jesus loves you and Monkey too.

Blain: Those are good predictions. Love you too monkey.

Monkey: Happy Nude Year!

Blain: It is 'New' Year.

Monkey: We will see.

Monkey: Blain, now that people can see me, sometimes, do they see me how you see me?

Blain: Nope, I've asked. They see either a capuchin or chimp.

Monkey: Whys is that? Chimps aren't even monkeys, they are apes.

Blain: I don't know, I don't make the rules. The difference between the two are if you are up to little trouble or big trouble. And correct! Chimps are not monkeys.

Monkey: How do you see me?

Blain: Depends on how you want to be seen and your mood.

Monkey: I can be more than a monkey...or an ape.

Blain: Really?

Monkey: I can be you too, or a hedgehog, bunny, dragon....

Blain: You can look like me?

Monkey: Yep, watch...

Blain: Freaky. Don't do that please.

Monkey: Bunny....Cat....Lizard.....Cartoon....

Monkey and Blain

Blain: Why do you usually choose a monkey….or ape?

Monkey: Dunno, I don't make the rules either.

Blain: I prefer the two that others can see.

Monkey: Dragon!

Blain: spooky.

Monkey: im gonna try to just relax and appear as whatever…..

Blain: Capuchin. Must be your natural state.

Monkey: MONKEY!

Blain: wait, now chimp.

Monkey: I just got a terrific idea…

Blain: Clearly not.

Monkey: Be back in a bit.

Monkey: Hey Blain, wanna hear a joke?

Blain: Clean joke or dirty joke?

Monkey: Clean Joke, I promise.

Blain: Ok, let's hear it.

Monkey: What did one snowman say to the other?

Blain: What?

Monkey: Do you smell carrots?

Blain: That is a pretty good one. Where did you hear it?

Monkey: Read it.

Blain: You can read?

Monkey: OF COURSE I CAN READ YOU CONDESCENDING JACKASS!

Blain: No need for name calling.

Monkey: You call me 'monkey'....speaking of that, why don't I have an actual name?

Blain: We went over this before. Only a crazy person would name an invisible imaginary monkey.

Monkey: However, talking to a nameless invisible monkey is perfectly sane.

Blain: Exactly, so I call you 'monkey'....basically your name IS monkey.

Monkey: Right....perfectly sane.....no worries there.....carry on.

Monkey on Blain's job/In DC, monkey's birthplace/travel

Monkey: Haven't gotten a single thing done, phone calls, got to get started, need to get started, gonna schedule out through the 20th, or something. Stupid travel day, stupid holiday, stupid briefing....rant rant rant...tomorrow is a new day...

Monkey: WINNING!!...ok, not really, but I am tired at 9pm, that is a plus, may sleep tonight, it has been 4 days, it should help, gotta catch that squirrel, got to, new week new week. Yep.

Monkey: You want 100% Completion? Well Great! It is good to want things. It teaches you disappointment.

Monkey: Donning my cape, mask and tights....Off to keep the nation safe! Ok, im wearing a suit and no cape or mask, but I AM wearing tights.

Monkey: Loud things, rumbling things, barking things, screaming things, sirens...bright things, flashing things, blinking things....fast moving things, strange looking things, jerky moving things...crowded spaces, empty places....go, go, go, go, go, wait, wait wait....gogogogogogoggogogo..... waaaaaaaaaaaaait. Not a big fan of our nation's capitol, ready to go home....with a 12 hour trip.

Monkey: What is Blain doing up at 222am DC time? Finishing! 100% Completion! That's right, rockstar, proofreading and admin stuff. Up and down. 12 hours travel and back in Iowa.

Blain: Please do not bother me today monkey, i need to get this typed.

IIM: Hey Blain?

Blain: Yes monkey?

IIM: You're welcome.

Blain: I'm done now, thank you monkey, lets go fling more poo.

IIM: YAYYYYYYYYYYYYYYY!

NEW MEXICO

Monkey: WE ATE A TOUCAN!

Blain: we did NOT!

Monkey: Taco places serve tacos, Pizza places serve pizza, Tocanos sells toucans...right?

Blain: No, we ate steak.

Monkey: Maaaaaaaan, I thought we had the 'follow your nose' bird.

Blain: Sorry, maybe tomorrow we can catch snakes.

Monkey: And eat them!

Blain: No.

Monkey: Bring them inside the hotel?

Blain: Maybe.

Monkey: Hot Diggity!

Monkey: Thought you didn't drink?

Blain: When a Vietnam vet-biker named 'Bones' tells you to try his moonshine, you try it.

Monkey: How was it?

Blain: Surprisingly smooth and tasty.

Monkey: Are you blind?

Blain: No, this was actual Tennessee Moonshine.

Monkey: Illegal?

Blain: Most likely.

Monkey: You drunk?

Blain: Nope, I only took a sip of each flavor.

Monkey: Was still like 4 of them.

Blain: I'll be ok.

Monkey: You're fault if you go blind.

Blain: I saw someone drink an entire jar of it yesterday.

Monkey: Did they go blind?

Blain: It was Bones.

Monkey: moonshine sauce!

CALIFORNIA

Monkey: What in the sunny crap is That Smell?

Blain: Skunk?

Monkey: Come on man, that would either be the biggest skunk in history or the town is covered with them.

Blain: Maybe it is just the air quality?

Monkey: Gross. California stinks.

Blain: Be thankful we are Iowans.

Monkey: Word.

Monkey: Hey Blain?

Blain: Yes?

Monkey: I got chocolate on the bed.

Blain: It isn't poop, right?

Monkey: Nope, really is chocolate.....this time.

Blain: Oh good. Wait, this time?

Monkey: Remember New Mexico?

Blain: Yeah?

Monkey: That was poop.

Blain: you are disgusting.

Monkey: This is true.

Monkey: Blain, you have work that came in.

Blain: Yeah?

Monkey: A case in....wait for it....wait for it....wait for it....

Blain: Just tell me.

Monkey: Afghanistan.

Blain: Pass.

GOVERNMENT

Monkey: I was reading a biography on Bonhoeffer. He was a german who participated in the assassination attempt on Hitler. He was also a pastor.

Blain: Yeah?

Monkey: Now, im not comparing President Obama to Hitler, however the scene in Germany right after WW1 and before Hitler was totally in control, described in the book, sounds a lot like America today.

Blain: That isn't good.

Monkey: Now, did I just call President Obama, Hitler? No. But America is about 1 step from Germany prior to WW1. Right place, right time and all that. China holds our markers and we are in a bad economic state. A charismatic person steps in, current leader, next leader, whoever, and they start to 'make things better'. Start providing programs for free assistance like healthcare and education.

Blain: Sounds Hitler-ish.

Monkey: So, this leader could publically say that Congress isn't doing their job, and 'temporarily' suspends them. The leader would have total power, but knows it wouldn't last long.

Blain: Fiction, right?

Monkey: During this period of total power, the leader abolishes Congress, making it permanent. Then the leader gets their own personal guards, again, not calling President Obama Hitler, this could be any future person also. But if this all happened, we could be Germany after WW1 and before WW2.

Blain: Scary thought.

Monkey: Concentration camps and world power. I think I'll go to bed.

Blain: Super. I think i'll stay up.

Monkey's public statement on Facebook gets redacted by government (not true for amusement purposes only)

Monkey: Know what's on my mind? I think that the ██, I'm also in the process of starting ████████████ ████████. So, in short it is true that we ████████

█████████████████████████████████. In further
news, don't ever █████████████████████████.

Portions of this public statement were redacted for YOUR protection. The person making these comments has been flagged and are under constant monitoring.

Monkey: Hey Blain, i googled, it so it's true, right?

Blain: Yep, that is how it works.

Monkey: Did you know that the democrats go their symbol of a donkey because people called Andrew Jackson a Jackass?

Blain: Well this should piss people off.

Monkey: The republicans got the elephant from a harper bazaar cartoon.

Blain: Ok?

Monkey: I had to know why, so I googled it. Kinda weird symbols if you ask me.

Blain: What would you choose?

Monkey: When I start my own political party, I'm gonna pick a fierce animal, like a lion.

Blain: Good choice.

Monkey: Or a T-Rex.

Blain: Stick with lion.

Monkey: Hey Blain? Do you think the people would like to be referred as the United Social States of America (USSA) or Western China?

Blain: Ha ha ha ha ha ha ha ha.

Monkey: Not looking good for the grand ole nation.

Blain: Can't live off pretend money.

Monkey: We got a plan?

Blain: Yep.

In 2012

Monkey: Im predicting a civil war coming to the US.

Blain: Why is that?

Monkey: It won't be a race war, it won't be a class war, not North vs South.

Blain: What are you talking about?

Monkey: It will be a political civil war. Republicans vs Democrats. Mark it on your calendars. People are being *BLEEP*s.

Blain: Nah.

Monkey: This nation has split. It's just a matter of time until the physical violence starts. Don't be a Jackass America! We do NOT war against ourselves.

good news about this 2012 prediction, as of 11/2019 there hasn't been rampant violence

Monkey: Thought of the day...We, well you, I'm imaginary, have Rights by God. They are Rights. Not laws, not privileges, they are Rights!

Blain: Ok. Established we have Rights.

Monkey: So, if someone takes your Rights, you are no longer free. If you are no longer free, you are a slave. Slavery is illegal.

Blain: True.

Monkey: Therefore, someone taking your Rights is an illegal act. If you give up your Rights, you are a fool. There is no other way to put it. If you don't give up your Rights, and someone tries to take your Rights, you have a duty to resist them,

Blain: Be careful here monkey.

Monkey: I got this. Any Rights, all Rights, we should resist from someone taking them. But understand what Rights actually are first.

Blain: You put it in a way that you aren't advocating for violence, right?

Monkey: Fo Sho. Non-violent steaksauce.

Monkey declares himself King of everything

Monkey: King Monkey's new rule, as of today: Warning labels only have to be on a product for the first 5 years the product is available to the public. Take all warning labels off any product that has been available over 5 years. Example

1) Coffee is usually served hot, unless ordered cold, and you have no right to sue if your coffee is 'too hot'. Example 2) Preparation H is for your butt, and only your butt. If you put it anywhere else, you get to live with the consequences, you may not sue. Example 3) Using corded electric devices in water is not a good idea. Unless you are under 5 years of age, you should know this by now, and you get to live...or not live with the consequences, you may not sue. If ignorance of the law is no excuse, then ignorance in general is also no excuse. This is why you humans have lost your common sense. Start thinking for yourselves. This has been your new ruler-King Monkey.

Blain: Sounds fair.

Monkey: Thus sayth the king.

Monkey: Hey Blain, did you know you are a racist, sexist, homophobe?

Blain: Well yeah, I'm a white male heterosexual.

Monkey: So you ARE all these?

Blain: Don't be a jackass. I'm a white male heterosexual only. People think that I have this thing called 'white privilege' and other nonsense.

Monkey: People making stuff up?

Blain: Yep, I forgive them though, they are all being manipulated by the media and government.

Monkey: What a bunch of *BLEEP*.

Blain: Totally. Oh, and it is NOT 'Merica, it is America.

Monkey: Want to hear me use a bunch of slang?

Blain: Not today monkey.

Political strife gets rough in President Obama's 2nd term making Blain's job difficult

Blain: Well, that went about as I expected.

Monkey: People hate the MAN.

Blain: The gun cocking sound from behind the door is quite the modivater.

Monkey: You move pretty fast for an old guy.

Blain: He said, 'last warning'. Didn't care about the badge or what I was doing there.

Monkey: But you are here to help and do good things.

Blain: Doesn't matter, people are pissed and I am the one in the field.

Monkey: Stay safe, be smart, be alert.

Blain: Roger Roger, on to the next one.

Blain: What did that envelope say?

Monkey: Something from the CDC. What is a CDC?

Blain: Center for disease control?

Monkey: Oops.

Blain: What?!?

Monkey: I ate the notice.

Blain: Why? Nevermind, did you read it first?

Monkey: Something something radiation, something something unclassified species, further tests.

Blain: That doesn't sound good.

Monkey: No worries, I took care of it.

Blain: You ate it!

Monkey: And now it is gone.

Blain: The FED is printing new money

Monkey: How do they do that?

Blain: They basically say that we need more money printed and do it.

Monkey: Sounds like a recipe for disaster.

Blain: Yes. We are also living off pretend money called credit.

Monkey: What happens if a massive electrical impulse wipes out the pretend money records?

Blain: Exactly. Dont worry about it, it's all ok. Be a good sheep, carry on, we got this.....we as in the government, not me and Monkey.

Monkey and Blain

Monkey: I'm not fixing *BLEEP*, I didn't break anything.

Blain: Me either, but be a helper.

Monkey: Fine! PSA FROM MONKEY: HEY PEOPLE, STOP SPENDING MONEY YOU DON'T HAVE, YOU TOO U.S. GOVERNMENT.

Blain: Thanks buddy, you are a helpful Monkey.

Monkey: Hey US Government, since we are borrowing money that we can't afford to pay back, I could use a free government grant of approximately $200000.00, Thanks.

Blain: You know they can't hear you, right?

Monkey: But I spoke right into your work computer.

Blain: Oh, then yes, they can hear you.

Monkey: Hashtag NSA, Hashtag Obama, Hashtag Government, Hashtag Socialist.

Blain: Quite verbal hashtagging, that is for the Internet.

Monkey: Oh.

Monkey tries again posting on Facebook

Monkey: I have a secret to tell you. The government ***COMMENT ERASED BY THE NSA*.** Can you believe that?

Blain: Will never get through.

Monkey: Let's find out.

Monkey: Hey Blain?

Blain: Yes monkey?

Monkey: I didn't understand a word that guy said on the phone.

Blain: Me either, should be a hoot!

Monkey: Can I drive this time?

Blain: Why not, that should be a hoot and a half.

Iowa

Monkey: Hey Blain, why are we sitting here in Dubuque?

Blain: I have 1 more appointment at 4pm.

Monkey: 4?!?! That is like an hour and a half away.

Blain: Yes, and?

Monkey: IMMMMMMM BOOOOORRRREEEDDD!

Blain: I have some typing to do while I wait.

Monkey: YOU have typing to do, I have nothing to do. I'm gonna sing songs.

Blain: If you be good, and you are quiet, I will let you drive home.

Monkey: For the whole time?

Blain: Yep, for the whole hour and a half.

Monkey: Ok, deal. We are gonna go off-roading though.

Blain: Stick to the roads and obey all traffic laws.

Monkey: Fine!

30 seconds later

Monkey: Hey Blain?

Blain: we have a deal monkey, quiet for an hour and a half so I can type.

Monkey: Ok, nevermind.

15 seconds later

Monkey: Hey Blain?

Blain: Monkey, I won't let you drive home if you keep interrupting me.

Monkey: But it is important this time.

Blain: What do you need Monkey.

Monkey: I have to pee.

Blain: Use a bottle.

Monkey: NO WAY! I'm not some beast.

Blain: I've done it, if you gotta go, you gotta go. You have the correct equipment.

Monkey: You have peed in a bottle? Gross!

Blain: Either go in the bottle or in your pants.

Monkey: No pants. Nekkid Monkey!

Blain: Just go in the bottle.

Monkey: Deep vein thrombosis!

Blain: Knock it off. I don't think that is what that means.

Monkey: FINE! I will pee in the bottle, then im gonna nap. Wake me so i can drive home.

Monkey: Blain, where are we?

Blain: West Union.

Monkey: Someone need money?

Blain: Not Western Union, West Union, IA.

Monkey: Where in the crap is that?

Blain: Not sure, I love GPS.

Monkey: Perv!

Blain: GPS is the fancy direction device that navigates me.

Monkey: OH! Then I love GPS too, and UPS, and CDO...

Blain: What is CDO?

Monkey: It's the same as OCD, but in alphabetical order, as it should be.

Blain: I can't argue with that.

Monkey and Blain

Monkey: Hey Blain?

Blain: Monkey, why are you always most active when I'm typing?

Monkey: Dunno. Hey Blain? Guess what I'm doing.

Blain: I don't know, what are you doing?

Monkey: I'm making brownies.

Blain: Where are you? You don't sound like you are in the kitchen.

Monkey: I'm not. I'm in the bathroom making brownies.

Blain: Gross!

Monkey: Just thought I would let you know.

Monkey: So I asked ██████████ at Fort Bragg if they were training for a zombie attack. I can neither confirm or deny that our military are preparing for a zombie attack.

Monkey: Hey Blain? Did that guy really say ██████████ ██████████?

Blain: Yep, good thing too.

Monkey: Heard that!

Blain: today was a better day, don't you agree?

Monkey: Yep, went smoother. Good thing too, I was about to open a can o' whoopass on ya.

Blain: You were?

Monkey: Yep. We are tough and capable. We can do anything.

Blain: Indeed. I need you to do something for me though.

Monkey: What's that?

Blain: Stop saluting everyone. It's a bit embarrassing. And stop telling people you were in 'Nam'.

Monkey: Oh. Ok....but this one time in 'Nam', we were deep in the jungle...

Blain: THAT's what I'm talking about. We are too young to have been in Vietnam.

Monkey: You maybe, but me, I was there, and we were deep in the jungle...and then the...

Blain: Stop, please stop.

Monkey: FINE! I won't tell you how it was in 'Nam'. Want to hear about Korea?

Blain: No monkey, not now. Be a good monkey.

***Saluting* Monkey:** YES SIR!

Monkey: Blain, your computer is racist.

Blain: Crap, what now monkey?

Monkey: Your computer does not recognize spanish words in spell check, every single one of them came up as misspelled.

Blain: That doesn't make my computer racist.

Monkey: It doesn't?

Blain: Nope, it means the computer doesn't know spanish.

Monkey: Well Rosetta Stone it or something.

Blain: I'm not allowed to install anything on this computer.

Monkey: Cause the aliens?

Blain: Yes monkey, cause of the aliens.

Monkey: That sucks.

North Carolina

Monkey: Blain!

Blain: Yes monkey?

Monkey: They can't blow up goats on Fort Bragg anymore.

Blain: What?

Monkey: No more blowing up goats on Fort Bragg.

Blain: What are you talking about? Who is blowing up goats?

Monkey: The Army was blowing up goats. They cant anymore.

Blain: Are you making this up?

Monkey: Nope, Fox News man, just read it, no more blowing

up goats.

Blain: You just like saying 'blowing up goats' don't you?

Monkey: Yep. There will be no more blowing up goats on Fort Bragg anymore.

Blain: I suppose that is good for the goats.

Monkey: Yep, good that the goats will not be blown up anymore.

Blain: Are you finished?

Monkey: Steaksauce! Ok, now I'm done.

Monkey: Hey Blain, are we doing landry....lawndry.....laundry...whatever, tomorrow?

Blain: Yes monkey.

Monkey: Can i ride in the dryer again?

Blain: again?

Monkey: I rode in the dryer last week, it was fun, like a swirling sauna.

Blain: you didn't make any mess on my clothes, did you?

Monkey: Nope. Vomit fee, poop free.

Blain: Then go for it, ride away....just don't be too loud. I think i will be doing the laundry at the hotel tomorrow. Don't want to spook the other guests.

Monkey: Usually not loud, I just giggle the whole time.

More of a chuckle/wheeze.

Blain: Knock yourself out. Happy laundry riding.

Monkey: YAYYYYY! Can I pee off the hotel roof?

Blain: Definitely out of the question.

Monkey: Thought I'd try to sneak one past you.

Blain: Good try, no peeing in public.

Monkey: Fine.

Blain: Get bored at home? Don't like where you live? Here is what you do....find a way to have your job send you somewhere for 1 month at a time. Same job, different area, for the entire month. Far enough away so you can't go home on weekends. Complete this month long experience then ask yourself if you like this new work plan. There is no place like home.

Monkey: Word.

Blain: no steaksauce?

Monkey: Steaksauce IS the word.....Steaksauce.

Blain: Knew you couldn't resist.

Monkey: Blain, what do you do for work?

Blain: Protect the nation from alien invasions.

Monkey: WHAT?!?!

Blain: Keeping the nation safe.

Monkey: Really?

Blain: No. I ask people a bunch of questions.

Monkey: You ask them if they are trouble makers?

Blain: Maybe, I'm not at liberty to say.

Monkey: Has anyone ever said 'yes sir, I'm a trouble maker.'?

Blain: Not yet.

Monkey: What do you do if they say yes?

Blain: No idea, hoping no one ever admits directly to me that they are a trouble maker.

Monkey: Cause you will have to whoop ass them?

Blain: No, because I'm not sure I can only do what I'm told to do.

Monkey: Too heavy man. Lets just tell people you are a dog whisperer or professional bigfoot hunter.

Blain: I actually tell people I sell insurance, guarantees no follow up questions.

Monkey: That works?

Blain: Yep, no one wants to buy insurance just off the cuff from a stranger.

Monkey: Good plan.

Blain: How is the book going?

Monkey: Check this out....'therefore those who win every battle are not really skillful-those who render others' armies helpless without fighting are the best of all.'

Blain: What exactly are you reading?

Monkey: 'The Art of War'.

Blain: Really?

Monkey: Yep, good interpersonal skills, not just war tactics.

Blain: Let me know how it turns out.

Monkey: steaksauce. STEAKSAUCE!

Blain: Weirdo.

Monkey: So I'm still in NC, watching 'Meet Joe Black' for the first time. Death likes peanut butter....Blain likes peanut butter....Im pretty sure Blain IS death. Just saying..... Steaksauce?

Blain: Hey monkey, what are you doing?

Monkey: Nothing dea....Blain.

Blain: Ok, just checking. Who were you talking to?

Monkey: Audio diary, good to remember things.

Blain: Ok. I'm gonna have a peanut butter sandwich, want one?

Monkey: No thanks, I'm good.

Monkey: Hey Blain?

Blain: Yes monkey?

Monkey: I took a photo with your phone.

Blain: Ok...

Monkey: I would like to discuss this photo.

Blain: Ok....what are your thoughts?

Monkey: If the fire is on the stairs wouldn't I want to use the elevator? Secondly, if the place is on fire and the sign says use the stairs, shouldn't there be no fire on the stairs?

Blain: I see your point. I think it is the aspergers.

Monkey: You're an asperger.

Blain: No need for name calling.

Monkey: This warning is just stupid.

Blain: What do you suggest?

Monkey: Same warning, but with a picture of the elevator on fire, not the stairs.

Blain: Write your congressperson.

Monkey: Wiseass, I'm serious, wouldn't children not use the stairs if the picture showed them on fire?

Blain: Why would children be at a hotel alone?

Monkey: Not the point!

Blain: What is the point?

Monkey and Blain

Monkey: This sign is stupid.

Blain: That's it?

Monkey: That's it.

Monkey: You look like someone poured snake blood in your eyes.

Blain: Yeah? That's not good.

Monkey: You look high.

Blain: How do you know what that looks like?

Monkey: I watch a lot of TV.

Blain: Man, do I really look that rough?

Monkey: Yep, hope you get some rest when you get home, I get concerned about you.

Blain: Really?

Monkey: No nancy, just trying to be helpful. I DO hope you can actually get some sleep though.

Blain: Me too. Good thing is I'm not hallucinating.

Monkey: Yet.

Blain: Yeah, Yet. But heading home on Friday, back to the frozen lands of Iowa.

Monkey: YAYYYYY! Steak Sauuuuuuuuuuuccccc. c. c. c. e!

Monkey: I pooped in the elevator at the hotel.

Blain: It is a 2 story hotel, why did you use the elevator?

Monkey: I needed to poop.

Blain: Anyone see you?

Monkey: Nope.

Blain: Then we will keep this quiet. Don't poop anywhere except the bathroom.

Monkey: I pooped in the lobby too.

Blain: Why?

Monkey: Again, had to poop.

Blain: We're going to get kicked out of this hotel.

Monkey: Good, then we can go home.

Blain: Not until the job is done.

Monkey: I want to go home.

Blain: I do too. This won't last forever.

Monkey: Feels like forever.

Blain: We are big, bad and tough. We can do this. Are we men or are we mice?

Monkey: I'm a monkey.

Blain: It's a saying.

Monkey: A stupid saying, L'm a monkey.

Blain: Ok....Are we monkeys or are we mice?

Monkey: What?

Blain: Nevermind. I want to go home too, but we can't. So we buckle down and get the job done, then we can go home.

Monkey: Promise?

Blain: Promise.

Monkey: Hey Blain?

Blain: Yes monkey?

Monkey: Did you know foreign citizens can join the US military?

Blain: Yep, why?

Monkey: How do you feel about that?

Blain: Kinda on the fence. Good for them to help the country out, but a great way to infiltrate the country's military.

Monkey: Good point. I liked the guy we met from Africa today.

Blain: Yeah?

Monkey: He was full of joy. Why aren't you filled with joy?

Blain: Dunno, maybe it is an African thing, I've never been to Africa.

Monkey: Nah, you are just a grumpy goat.

Blain: True.

Monkey: Steaksauce.

Monkey: What did that guy ask you?

Blain: If I smoked.

Monkey: Weren't you outside smoking when he asked?

Blain: Yeah, but he meant smoke pot.

Monkey: So that guy clearly has no idea what you do for a living.

Blain: I don't advertise.

Monkey: Guess you look like a pothead then.

Blain: Guess so. He was the second stranger to ask about drugs on this trip.

Monkey: Yep, you look like a pothead.

Blain: It is probably because I talk to you. People don't see you, remember?

Monkey: Sure, blame the monkey.

Blain: Or because I look like a pothead.

Monkey: I think so.

Blain: Well, you look like a….a….. I got nothing.

Monkey: Probably all that weed, killing your brain cells.

Blain: I don't smoke pot.

Monkey: UmmmmHmmmm.

Blain: Monkey, you are always with me, when would I smoke pot?

Monkey: I DO sleep sometimes.

Blain: Whatever.

Monkey: Whatever.........pothead.

Monkey: Hey Blain, how many old ladies does it take to fax 1 form?

Blain: Be nice monkey.

Monkey: Fine! Hey Blain? Did you see that leopard rat today?

Blain: It was a chipmunk.

Monkey: Couldn't have been. Chipmunks wear clothes and sing songs, it was a leopard rat.

Blain: Ok, then yes, i saw the leopard rat.

Monkey: I caught it and brought it inside. It is in the drawer.

Blain: It better not be monkey.

Monkey: Yep, I put it in my pocket.

Blain: You don't have pockets.

Monkey: Ok, I carried it in my mouth.

Blain: Gross.

Monkey: Leopard rat sauce!

Monkey: 'Moves like Jagger' is a Maroon 5 song.

Blain: Finally looked it up?

Monkey: Yep, wanted to make sure it wasn't someone weird.

Blain: Super.

Monkey: Gangnam style is more than a pistachio commercial....it is a real song.

Blain: You have to be kidding.

Monkey: Dance is part of it too.

Blain: Of course, Monty Python invisible horse riders would be proud.

Monkey: I still don't know what the harlem shake is.

Blain: I don't really care.

Monkey: Turns out I don't either.

Monkey: LET'S DO THAT AGAIN!

Blain: No.

Monkey: But it was hilar....haliro....very very funny.

Blain: No.

Monkey: You suck!

Monkey and Blain

Blain: steaksauce?

Blain: Well it's good thing im not busy.

Monkey: Sounds like sarcasm, what's up buttercup?

Blain: I have to take 2 forced days off from work.

Monkey: Paid?

Blain: Yes.

Monkey: Then....WOO HOO! Days off!

Blain: But i have deadlines, and have to work harder in shorter amount of time and faster and still take the time off.

Monkey: So Basically, you have the same amount of work, less time to do it, get 2 days off, and still have to make sure the deadlines are met?

Blain: Yes.

Monkey: Well that is a bunch of *BLEEP*....Still have the censor button i see.

Blain: Yes it is, and yes i do. You swear too much.

Monkey: Good thing you aren't busy. So what are we gonna do on the days off?

Blain: Babysit plumbers and carpenters.

Monkey: *BLEEP* More house stuff?

Blain: Yep.

Monkey: You should just quit your job.

Blain: Yeah? And then what?

Monkey: Build guitars.

Blain: Can't make a living at it.

Monkey: Write a book.

Blain: I thought you were taking the lead on that.

Monkey: .....Im out of ideas for you.

Blain: Me too. So until then....Working for the Man every night and day.

Monkey: That should be in a song.

Blain: It is.

Monkey: I got moves like a jaguar, moves like a jaguar.

Blain: Close. Just cause you now know who sings that doesn't mean you have to sing it constantly.

Monkey: Booooooo. Go do laundry.

Blain: You go do laundry.

Monkey: I can be naked, you can't.

Blain: Fine! I'll go do laundry.

Monkey: WINNNNNN!

Monkey: ......and i was all like 'blam blam blam' and shot the dude.

Blain: WHAT?!?!?

Monkey: oh, you know....'blam blam blam' steaksauce.

Blain: annnnnnnnnnnnnnnnnnnd done for the week!

Monkey: YAYYYYYYY! Can we poop out the window?

Blain: no.

Monkey: Can we climb the statue and take photos?

Blain: Maybe, but we might get arrested. That would be hard to explain while out of town.

Monkey: Can we eat pizza?

Blain: THAT we can do with no risk of arrest.

Monkey: Watch me!

Blain: Monkey! No.

Monkey: Blain, I'm bored.

Blain: Go rent a movie.

Monkey: You go rent a movie, it freaks people out when I do it.

Blain: True, but we could film it and sell it, make millions, it would be awesome!

Monkey: So the plan is to get placed into a mental hospital this weekend?

Blain: Ok, maybe not a good idea.

Monkey: We could go to Walmart and get laundry detergent.

Blain: Why?

Monkey: To do laundry you donkey.

Blain: Right. I thought maybe you were planning something naughty.

Monkey: Always.

Blain: I so do NOT want to type this big stinky report.

Monkey: Whaaa? We are gonna eat a big stinky report?

Blain: No, TYPE a big stinky report.

Monkey: We haaatttteeeessss big stinky reports.

Blain: Why are you doing that?

Monkey: Doing what? WE HAAAATTTESSS YOUUUUU!

Blain: THAT! Stop doing that!

Monkey: Is reports crunchy or chewy?

Blain: I'm up to speed now, you are being Golem….pretty good impression.

Monkey: WE HATES BIG STINKY REPORTS FOREVER!….That guy cracks me up. Hey Blain, can we get a Golem, keep him as a pet?

Blain: No.

Monkey: Whyyyyyyyy?

Blain: He isn't real, he doesn't exist.

Monkey: I don't exactly exist either, but here I am.

Blain: True, but the answer is still no.

Monkey: WE HATES BLAIN FOREVERRRR! Precious....where's my precious?

Blain: Go watch a movie or something, I need to type the big stinky report.

Monkey: YAYYYYY, I LOVES BLAIN FOREVERRRR! And movies, and pizza, and....

Blain: yes, yes, yes, carry on Monkey. I need to type.

Monkey: precious-sauce.

Blain: 10 hours in a suit in 90 degree weather.

Monkey: Two bunnies in the backyard. Pineapples.

Blain: yep

Monkey: An interesting thing happened on the way to the office today.

Blain: Yeah?

Monkey: Yeah.

Blain: That's it?

Monkey: Yeah.

Blain: You are supposed to tell what interesting thing happened when you start a story like that.

Monkey: Oh sorry. Nothing interesting thing happened on the way to the office today.

Blain: That's better, but it is a lot like saying 'I didn't see a Unicorn today', unless you saw one on a previous days.

Monkey: Your rules suck.

Blain: Don't hate the player, hate the game.

Monkey: This game sucks too!

Monkey: BLAAAAAAAAAAAAAAAAINNNNN, IM BORRRR-RRREEEEED!

Blain: I need to get this report typed, got to get it done, got to get it done.....lets watch a movie instead....No, i need to get the report done.

Monkey: YAYYYYYYYYYY! Wait, BOOOOOOOOO!

5 minutes later

Monkey: Are you done yet?

3 minutes later

Monkey: Are you done yet?

7 minutes later

Monkey: Are you done yet?

1 minute later

Monkey: Are you done yet?

Blain: There comes a point on every TDY that my mind just starts to crack and im so ready to go home. Well, today is the day! I'm ready to go home, 4 days of work left, 1 travel day left.....I can do this!

Monkey: You sure there princess?

Blain: We should watch movies and eat pizza.

Monkey: I totally apologize for the 'princess' thing then.

Blain: Bet you do.

Monkey: Blain, I don't want to go to work today.

Blain: Too bad, rise and shine monkey!

Monkey: But I'm tired, and my head hurts, and I'm cold.

Blain: We have important stuff to do!

Monkey: But I don't want to.

Blain: GET UP! Are we men or are we mice?

Monkey: That again? I'm a monkey, and im going back to bed.

Blain: I'm heading out of town....

Monkey: Yeah?

Blain: I'll let you drive.....

Monkey: Yeah?

Blain: I will get you ice cream....

Monkey: Let's GO!

Blain: I need to shower first.

Monkey: You shower, I will warm up the car.

Blain: THAT'S the spirit!

Monkey: Ice Cream!

Blain: Whatever works.

Monkey: Hey Blain?

Blain: Yes monkey?

Monkey: Why don't people call you back when you leave messages?

Blain: Dunno, maybe they are busy.

Monkey: They suck...oops, I mean stink, still working on that.

Blain: I appreciate you trying to keep it clean, but in this case, you were right. I can't just sit around and wait for them to call back, let's make flapjacks!

Monkey: YESSSSSSSSSSSSSSSSS!

Blain: Always a good day when my report contains the word 'testicles'.

Monkey: What part of your report would need the word 'testicles'?

Blain: Reason for the police record.

Monkey: Exposed their...?

Blain: No, was kicked in the 'testicles'.

Monkey: Ouch, valid police record.

Blain: Indeed.

Blain: Sometimes I wish I was still PI.

Monkey: Why?

Blain: You get to wear what you want to blend in. But you won't believe the service that you get when wearing a suit.

Monkey: Kinda crappy for people not in suits.

Blain: True, shouldn't be treated differently. The badge helps too, but most people respect the suit.

Monkey: Fancy dancing.

Monkey: Regional?

Blain: Word.

Monkey: You sure?

Blain: I got an email and everything.

Monkey: Nice!

Blain: Thanks.

Monkey: Ice cream?

Blain: Nah, go ahead though, we earned it.

Monkey: YAYYYYYYYYYYYYYY!

Blain: Yet again, another report containing the word "testicles".

Monkey: Dang people, stop kicking each other in the nuts!

Blain: Can't use the word 'nuts' in the report, needs to be 'testicles'.

Monkey: Report would be shorter if you said 'nuts'.

15 DAYS OF CHRISTMAS/HOLIDAYS

Monkey: On the 1st day of Christmas my true love gave to me, some pudding in a fig tree.

Blain: I think you are mixing songs.

Monkey and Blain

Monkey: No one asked you.

Blain: Carry on.

Monkey: On the 2nd day of Christmas my true love gave to me, 2 ponds of ducks, and some pudding in a fig tree.

Blain: No comment.

Monkey: Yeah, shut it! I'm singing about Christmas.

Monkey: On the 4th day of Christmas my true love gave to me...

Blain: You missed the 3rd day.

Monkey: Crap...On the 3rd day of Christmas my true love gave to me, three french hens, two ponds of ducks and some pudding in a palm tree.

Blain: At least you day 3 correct.

Monkey: SILENCE!

Monkey: On the 4th day of Christmas my true love gave to me, four lizards laughing, three french horns, two ninja turtles, and some pudding in a fig tree.

Blain: Close enough.

Monkey: no wait, i messed that one up....On the 4th day of Christmas my true love gave to me, four calming birds, three french horns, two ninja turtles, and some pudding in a fruit tree. The lizards laughing is day 10.

Blain: Of course.

Monkey: Right on!

Monkey: On the 5th day of Christmas my true love gave to me, fiiiiiiiivvvvveeee goooooolllldddddeeennn riiiiiiinnnnngssssss!, like the Olympics, four calming...

Blain: The Olympics has 7 rings.

Monkey: Wait, what?

Blain: 7 rings.

Monkey: Then what is 5?

Blain: Golden rings.

Monkey: That's what I said.

Blain: The Olympics has 7 rings.

Monkey: STOP INTRUPTING ME!...fiiiiiiiiiiiiiiiiiiiv-vvvvvvvveeeeeee gooooooooooooolddddddennnnnnn riiiiiiiinnnnnnnnnngssssssssss, not like the Olympics which has 7 rings, four calming birds, three french hens, two pounds of duck, and a portrait of a little purple tree.

Monkey: Blain? What day am i on?

Blain: Does it matter?

Monkey: Don't be a scrooge Blain.

Monkey and Blain

Blain: 6. You are on day 6.

Monkey: Love you....On the 6th day of Christmas my true love gave to me, six sheep a swimming, fiiiiiiiivvvvvvvvvveeeeeee gollllllllllddddddddeeennnnnnn riiiiiiiinnnnnnggggggsssss, Olympics, four talking birds, three french hams, two fuzzy ducks, and some pudding cups under a tree.

Monkey: On the 7th day of Christmas God rested. Six sheep a swimming, fivvvvvvvvveeeeeee gooooolllllllddeeennnnnn riiiiiiiinnnnnnnngsssssss, four calming birds, three french horns, two little dogs, and some pudding in a pear tree.

Blain: Like I said, close enough.

Monkey: 162 days left!

Blain: You're kidding, right?

Monkey: Yeah I'm kidding, everyone knows there are only 15 days of Christmas.

Blain: Again, close enough.

Monkey: Steaksauce.

Monkey: On the 8th day of Christmas my true love gave to me, eight reindeer playing, seventh day God rested, six sheep a swimming, fiiiiiivvvvvvveeeeee gooooollllllldennnnn rinnnngggggggsssssss, OLYMPICS!, four calming birds, three french hens, two turquoise trucks, and some porridge in a plum tree.

Blain: 15 days?!?!?!? Really?!?!?

Monkey: Quit being a hater.

Blain: There are only 12 days of Christmas.

Monkey: Not anymore! It's Christmastime, quit being a poop.

Blain: Fine. Please continue.

Monkey: On the 9th day of Christmas my true love gave to me, nine types of cheeses, eight reindeer sleeping, seventh day God rested, six sheep a bleating, fiiiiiiiivvvvvvvvveeeeeeeeee gollllllllllllddddddddddeeeeeeeennnnnn nn fiiiiigs, four clucking birds, three french hens, two turtle eggs, and pudding sitting on the T.V.

Monkey: On the 10th day of Christmas my true love gave to me, ten lizards laughing, nine kinds of cheeses, eight reindeer poopin, seventh day God rested, six sheep for shearing, fiiiiiiiiivvvvvvvvvvvveeeeeeee gooooooollllllllddddddennnnn teeeeeeeeeettttttthhhhhh, four walking birds, three french horns, two fuzzy ducks, and some pudding on a fig tree.

Monkey: On the 11th day of Christmas my true love gave to me, eleven thumpers thumping, ten lizards laughing, nine kinds of cheeses, eight reindeer dancing, seventh day God rested, six sheep a swimming, fiiiiiiivvvvvvvvvvvveeeeeeee gooooooollllllllddddddddeeen riiiiiiiinnnnnnnggggs, olympics, four calling cards, three french pens, two plates of duck, and some pudding poured upon a peach tree.

Monkey: On the 11th day of Christmas my true love gave to me, twelve lords a leaping, eleven ladies dancing, ten pipers piping, nine drummers drumming, eight maids a milking, seven swans a swimming, six geese a laying, fiiiiivvvvvvvveeeeeee gooooooolllllllddddddeeeeennnn riiiiiinnnnnnggggggsss, four calling birds, three french hens, two turtle doves, and a partridge in a per tree.

Blain: Holy crap, I think those are actually right.

Monkey: Of course it's right, I've been messing it up to screw with you.

Blain: Not cool monkey.

Monkey: I thought it was funny.....On the 13th day of Christmas....

Blain: Are you really doing 15 days?

Monkey: Yep, I'm doing all 15 days!

Monkey: On the 13th day of Christmas my true love gave to me, thirteen screaming children, twelve pounds of bacon, eleven feet of duct tape, ten lizards laughing, nine types of steaksauce, eight reindeer leaping, seventh day God rested, six sheep a 'baaaaaaaaa'ing, fiiiiiivvvvvvveeeee goooo ooooooolllllddddddeeeeeennnnnnn riiiiiinnnggggggggsssssss, four talking birds, three french horns, two purple ducks and some pudding pops in a little tree.

Blain: Ok, you are really ending on 15?

Monkey: Yep.

Blain: Carry on.

Monkey: On the 14th day of Christmas my true love gave to me, fourteen pairs of meggings, thirteen crying children, twelve rabbits humping, eleven bells a ringing, ten lizards sleeping, nine bags of licorice, eight reindeer pooping, seventh day God rested, six sheep a skipping, fiiiiiiivvvvvvvvvvvveeeeeeee goooollllllllldennnnnnnnn pppppppeeeeeeaaaaaaaassssssss, four waddling ducks, three french hens, two quacking ducks, and an old box of crayons in a pudding tree.

Blain: Last one?

Monkey: 15 Blain, pay attention!

Monkey: On the 15th day of Christmas my true love gave to me, fifteen balls a bouncing, fourteen pairs of meggings, twelve little bunnies...

Blain: You missed thirteen.

Monkey: Nope, sent the brats home. Twelve little bunnies, eleven kinds of fungus, ten creepy lizards, nine wheel of cheeses, eight farting reindeer, seventh day God rested, six sheep a hustling, fiiiiiiiivvvvvvvvvveeeeeeee goooooooolll llllldddddddennnnnnnnnn teeeeeeeeeeefffff (Gangsta), four types of birds, three french horns, two pickle spears and my own show on cable T.V!!!!!!!!

Monkey and Blain

Blain: Nice ending!

Monkey: Yeah Dog!

Blain: Stop.

Monkey: Monkey Steaksauce everybody!

IIM: Hey Blain?

Blain: Yes Monkey?

IIM: Can i have turkey?

Blain: Yes, why wouldn't you?

IIM: Just checking.

Blain: Happy Thanksgiving from IIM and Blain.

Monkey: Blain, want to hear a Thanksgiving joke?

Blain: Sure.

Monkey: What sound does a 1 legged turkey make?

Blain: I don't know, what sound does a 1 legged turkey make?

Monkey: Wobble Wobble. Happy Thanksgiving People!

Blain: A tad lame.

Monkey: A tad. Steaksauce!

Monkey: HAPPY CHRISTMAS!

Blain: That was yesterday.

Monkey: I know, but you kept me locked in that cage all yesterday, so I couldn't tell people yesterday.

Blain: I locked you in the cage because you said you were going to turn into a were-monkey.

Monkey: I make stuff up. Your dog pooped in the cage by the way.

Blain: Bit you in the butt yesterday, didn't it? We don't have a dog.

Monkey: Well played human. Don't worry, i will repay. I may have pooped in the cage.

Blain: Repay yourself.

Monkey: HmmmmF.

Monkey: We hurry through holidays.

Blain: You mean the Halloween directly to Christmas thing?

Monkey: Christmas before Halloween.

Blain: No way.

Monkey: Saw Halloween costumes and Christmas trees out at the same time.

Blain: This is true.

Monkey: Keeps getting earlier and earlier.

Blain: Maybe in 10 years it will lap itself and be back to normal.

Monkey: People are just in too much of a hurry.

Blain: Back to school sales in January.

Monkey: It has passed just holidays, just sales events.

Blain: Consumers.

Monkey: We need to take a pause.

Blain: Merry Christmas Everyone! (dated 10/19/2013)

IIM: What's up buttercup?

Blain: Not much, just watching some TV.

IIM: Soooooo...

Blain: Yes monkey?

IIM: I don't understand Christmas.

Blain: Which part? It is the day we celebrate Jesus' birthday.

IIM: Why all the sales then?

Blain: Because we have forgotten why we celebrate Christmas.

IIM: Any why do i have to figure out what someone else wants as a gift?

Blain: Dunno monkey, I have never been able to do that.

IIM: Cause you are a sociopath?

Blain: Yep, and it makes me sad.

IIM: A sad sociopath? Is that possible?

Blain: Dunno. I guess I just get frustrated, then irritated, then overwhelmed because I don't understand it.

IIM: So I don't understand Christmas because You don't understand it?

Blain: I guess so.

IIM: Anyway, we should get our picture together for a card or something.

Blain: You think so?

IIM: Yep, I also think we should poop in the....

Blain: Nope. I will cut you off right there, we are not pooping in things and doing stuff with it.

IIM: Want to get the zombie preparedness bag ready?

Blain: Sounds like a plan, world ends in 26 days, suppose we should get something ready.

11/26/2012

Blain: I just realized I have Monday off.

Monkey: What for?

Blain: It is Columbus day. I don't get Easter, but darn it, Columbus day it is.

Monkey: Who is Columbus?

Blain: Was. He is dead. The guy who stole America from the Natives for Spain and Italy.

Monkey: Ooooooooo K.

Blain: Yep. He discovered 'India' that is why we are Indians. He also invented smooth jazz and velcro.

Monkey: Really?!?

Blain: No.

SOME OF MONKEY'S FAVORITE QUOTES, PARAPHRASED

Friendship is like peeing on yourself: Everyone can see it, but only you get the warm wetness in your pants. **Robert Bloch**

I don't want to die without scars. Only after disaster we are resurrected. After you've lost everything you're free to do anything. **Tyler Durden**

"Science investigates; religion interprets. Science gives man knowledge, which is power; religion gives man wisdom, which is control. Science deals mainly with facts; religion deals mainly with values. The two are not rivals." **Martin Luther King, actual quote.**

The reason that the road is long is because it takes a while to make your courage strong. **NeedToBreathe-Hard Love**

Stop burning down forests karen! **Smokey the Bear**

Wanting to change the world, but not yourself....lame. **Leo Tolstoy**

The beginning of something is always a little scary, but all great things do, right? **unknown**

I'm not a psychopath, psychopaths kill people for no reason. I kill people for money....that didn't come out right. **Martin Q Blank**

Be alone. That is the secret of invention. The best ideas come when alone. **Nikola Tesla**

Just like the hungry, pity the minds that don't eat also. **Victor Hugo**

Stay close to what makes you love life. **unknown**

Love God, Love people. **Yeshua**

PHILOSOPHY BY MONKEY

Monkey: Hey Blain.

Blain: What's up?

Monkey: I just got my Doctorate.

Blain: You did?

Monkey: Yep, I am Dr. Monkey now.

Blain: Is it ok if i just call you 'monkey' still?

Monkey: Yeah, it's not like im a General or something.

Blain: Nope, but you are a Major.

Monkey: Pain in the a....

Blain: No swearing.

Monkey: Was gonna say aspergers, dang.

Blain: Oh sorry, I jumped the gun.

Monkey: It's all good.

Blain: So are you a medical doctor now?

Monkey: No way, don't like blood. I got my Doctorate in Philosophy.

Blain: Nice job. Gonna teach or something?

Monkey: Nope, probably just gonna mooch off you.

Blain: Never gonna grow up?

Monkey: NO WAY. MAGIC BANANAS!

Monkey: Using order to deal with the disorderly, using calm to deal with the clamorous, is mastering the heart.

Blain: What?

Monkey: Reading.

Blain: Must be a pretty deep book.

Monkey: Something about the sun and formless water, being calm and doing things before they become immediately necessary.

Blain: What?!?

Monkey: It is a book. A booooooooook. Pages put together with a cover....and it's all about similar things by topic.

Blain: I know what a book is monkey. What is it about?

Monkey: I told you, formless water and the sun and stuff.

Blain: Just started it, didnt you.

Monkey: Yep. I'll let you know how it goes. Steaksauce.

Blain: Why do you keep saying steaksauce?

Monkey: Saw it on a TV show, thought it was funny.

Blain: Carry on then.

Monkey and Blain

Monkey: Blain, I think that Earth is not round.

Blain: Why is that? Read it on the Internet?

Monkey: No I didn't read it on the internet.

Blain: Ok, drop some knowledge on me.

Monkey: Ok. So I think the Earth is Oblong, like a capsule shape.

Blain: Ok. Why?

Monkey: Here it is, follow me on this. We start in Iowa. We can travel west, all the way around the Earth and end up back in Iowa. Same as for traveling east. 1 direction the whole way.

Blain: Ok.

Monkey: If we travel north, we go north, then south, then north again back to Iowa.

Blain: Weird.

Monkey: See? Oblong.

Blain: North and South are real directions and East and West are subjective.

Monkey: Right! Mind Blower!

Blain: I think we need to tell someone about this....Books and maps are wrong, all LIES!

Monkey: Settle down Blain, it was just a thought.

Blain: I may not be able to sleep now!

Monkey: Are you being a wiseass?

Blain: A little, but it was still a deep thought.

Monkey: Yeah, im a deep thinker.

Blain: Steaksauce.

Monkey: Ordinary people seem not to realize that those who really apply themselves in the right way to philosophy are directly and of their own accord preparing themselves for dying and death.

Blain: Wow, that was deep.

Monkey: I didn't think it up, it is Socrates.

Blain: Just pondering then?

Monkey: What good is my Doctorate in philosophy if i don't regurgitate other people's ideas and sayings to sound impressive and wise?

Blain: True.

Monkey: Want a true monkeyism?

Blain: Hit me with it Captain Fancypants.

Monkey: Money is dirt.

Blain: That's it?

Monkey: That's it....Money is dirt. Let it sink in, savour it, grasp it.

Blain: Have you been drinking?

Monkey: Nope. Just saying.

Blain: Saying what exactly?

Monkey: That money is dirt.

Blain: Steaksauce?

Monkey: Steaksauce.

Monkey: Want a few more monkeyisms?

Blain: I'm not sure.

Monkey: Come on, these are gold!

Blain: Ok, tell me more.

Monkey: You can't argue with crazy, crazy will grab you by the face and bite off your nose.

Blain: I agree with that one.

Monkey: I'm the kind of person that strangers want to hang out with. Be that type of person.

Blain: Another pretty good one.

Monkey: I can shape time and space with my mind.

Blain: See 'saying 1'?

Monkey: I can, you just need to learn to harness your powers....but shhhhh, don't let anyone know.

Blain: What?

Monkey: Crap, it slipped out....RISE UP MY PEOPLE!

Blain: What are you talking about?

Monkey: Nothing......Monkey revolution is coming.

Monkey: Blain.

Blain: Yes monkey?

Monkey: Assess the advantages in taking advice, then structure your forces accordingly, to supplement extraordinary tactics. Forces are to be structured strategically, based on what is advantageous.

Blain: More wisdom from the formless sun book?

Monkey: Yep. The author is Sun, the book is about knowing but being unknown and formlessness.

Blain: What?

Monkey: Not sure yet, still reading it. How did today go?

Blain: No terrible, worked only 4.5 hours today.

Monkey: Then why do you still look like you are crushing coal in your butt and making diamonds?

Blain: A consistent feeling of failure. Just waiting on reports to come back.

Monkey: But you finished it all. Worked like 50 hours this week, didnt you?

Blain: 49.

Monkey: Then let it go, watch some TV, have a hot bath.

Blain: Sage advice, I think the book is helping you.

Monkey: Word! Steaksauce.

Monkey: Blain, what do you want in life?

Blain: All I want is a peaceful soul.

Monkey: Dang! Deep!

Blain: It's true, i would trade anything i have for a peaceful soul.

Monkey: How about in the meantime we take a couple million dollars.

Blain: That would work for me, peaceful soul is a long time coming.

Monkey: Aliens?

Blain: Aliens.

Monkey: I'm not a fan of the whole 'keep calm and...' stuff.

Blain: Why not? Calmness is good.

Monkey: It is stupid. Maybe I don't want to keep calm. Keeping calm and doing nothing is rarely a good idea.

Blain: Silence is complanency....only thing that evil can triumph is for good people to do nothing and all that.

Monkey: Or to misquote a movie that I don't remember the title 'I'm as mad as hell and I'm not gonna take it anymore!'.

Blain: Time to act?

Monkey: May cause some loss of peacefulness.

Blain: Times of action usually are.

Monkey: MOUNT UP!

LIMERICK

Monkey: I know a fellow named Blain,

He is positively insane,

He talks to a monkey, smells like a donkey,

Possibly has squirrels in his brain.

Blain: That hurts my feelings.

Monkey: you don't have feelings.

Blain: wont stop me from whooping your butt.

Monkey: OOOOOOHHHH promises.

Blain: You will have to sleep some time.

Monkey: Crap, right. Im sorry....it was funny though.

Blain: it was pretty funny.

Yardwork

Monkey: Hey Blain, who rakes the forests?

Blain: What?

Monkey: Who is responsible for raking the leaves in a forest?

Blain: No one, the leaves just stay on the ground.

Monkey: Why in the crap do we have to rake at home?

Blain: Not sure, don't know if it is the law, or just expected by the neighbors.

Monkey: This is CRAP! Down with the MAN!

Blain: You get to use the leaf blower, I'm the one raking.

Monkey: Oh, right! I CONTROL THE WIND!

Blain: That's right! It is like a super power.

Monkey: SUPER MONKEY!

Blain: That's the spirit!

Monkey: I'm pretty sure i just got 'Tom Sawyered'.

Blain: maybe just a little.

Monkey: Raking leaves and cutting the lawn causes global warming.

Blain: Have any proof?

Monkey: Humans have been doing it for over 100 years,

and here we are.

Blain: Works for me.

Monkey: Raking sucks.

Blain: True that.

Monkey: Shovelling too.

Blain: Preach!

Monkey: Sing me a song choir boy.

Blain: It is an expression.

Monkey: Kinda like 'go f..

Blain: MONKEY!

Monkey: I was gonna say 'go fly a kite'.

Blain: Oh. Sorry.

Monkey: Potty mouth.

Blain: Guilty.

Monkey: Im done raking.

Blain: Me too.

Monkey: WOOF, you smell maximum real bro.

Blain: Thanks, worked on it.

Monkey: Seriously, you stink.

Blain: Want a hug?

Monkey: NOOOOOOOOOOOOOOOOOOOOOOOOOOOOOO! GO SHOWER!

Blain: Come on, want to cuddle?

Monkey: Go away stinky.

Earth/Climate Change

Monkey: I had a conversation with Earth today.

Blain: Yeah? How is Earth?

Monkey: First of all, Earth's name is actually Bill. No one bothered to ask before.

Blain: Interesting...

Monkey: Bill told me the truth about global warming/climate change.

Blain: Do tell.

Monkey: Bill is old, Bill is tired, Bill is dying. Bill also does not like humans and is trying to make them as miserable as possible before he dies completely.

Blain: Sounds accurate.

Monkey: Bill and I made an agreement. If the humans of earth will all give me, Monkey of Danland, $1.00 each, or a total of $7 Billion, then Bill will stop his punishment of the humans....until I die.

Blain: MONKEY!!

Monkey: After I die, its game back on...see ya suckas, kiss your butts goodbye. For a complete stop of Bill harming the humans, i can name a successor as the protector of Bill.

Blain: MONKEY!

Monkey: Up to you all, good luck.

Blain: I'm pretty sure this is a scam....a pretty well thought out scam, but still a scam.

Monkey: Risk it! Test Bill!

Blain: Here is my dollar.

Monkey: YESSSSSSSS! $6,999,999,999 to go!

Monkey: Climate Change insurance!

Blain: What?

Monkey: I will sell Climate Change insurance?

Blain: What happened to the zombie insurance?

Monkey: That is old thinking. Climate Change is the future!

Blain: Ok, I'll bite. Explain the new plan.

Monkey: Offer Climate Change insurance, probably U.S. based only. Collect premiums for 10 year coverage, 50 years coverage and 100 year coverage.

Blain: This sounds like another scam.

Monkey: The short ones are the most expensive. The 100 year ones are the least, but people don't live 100 years and they are non-transferable.

Blain: Sneaky. What happens if Climate Change kills a bunch of people.

Monkey: Word it so that there needs to be listed on the death certificate that the cause of death was 'Climate Change'.

Blain: Pretty sure this is illegal also.

Monkey: Gonna make millions off scared people.

Blain: Careful, governments don't like to share.

Monkey: MILLIONS!

Blain: I'm pretty sure this one will work, and that we will end up in jail.

Monkey: YES!

Blain: Set it up.

Bottled water/Government

Monkey: Do you think the government is pissed with so many bottled water brands?

Blain: From the plastic?

Monkey and Blain Diebolt

Monkey: No, because they cant put the mind altering chemicals in it like they do in the tap water.

Blain: What if the government secretly owns all the bottled water companies too?

Monkey: Oh man!

Blain: Calm down monkey, i was messing around.

Monkey: So you agree that the government has put mind altering chemicals in the tap water?

Blain: Didn't say that….I'm going to grab a bottle of water, want one?

Monkey: Sure…Who owns this fancy water anyway?

Blain: Pretty sure it is just bottled tap water.

Monkey: *spits it out* WHAT?!?!?!

Blain: Just kidding, i have no idea.

Monkey: turd.

Monkey: Blain, The ▆▆▆ in the ▆▆▆ is really ▆▆▆. Many times ▆▆▆ through ▆▆▆ ▆▆▆ and also ▆▆▆ ▆▆▆.

Blain: I don't think we can talk about this.

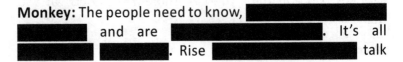

Monkey: The people need to know, ▆▆▆ ▆▆▆ and are ▆▆▆. It's all ▆▆▆ ▆▆▆. Rise ▆▆▆ talk

Monkey and Blain

████████████████. .

Blain: Seriously, we are going to be taken into custody if people heard.

Monkey: BLAIN! People need to know ████████ a ████████████ the price ████████ ████████. The ████████████ have ████████ ████████!

Blain: Yep, were going to Gitmo.

Portions of this conversation have been redacted by law

Monkey: Hanged by his neck until dead.

Blain: Until dead? Not just a little bit?

Monkey: Yep, until dead.

Blain: I always assumed that the hanging part was til death.

Monkey: Hanged by their feet til sick!

Blain: Yeah.

Monkey: Hanged by their peni.....

Blain: MONKEY!

Monkey: Fine! Hanged by their necks til dead.....cause they can take our lives, but they can never take our FREEEEEEDDDDOOOOMMMM!

Blain: Is that right william?

Monkey: Steaksauce.

Monkey gets censored

IIM: %*@#&*(&*($ @@%%&*#$**(*$ @@#^&**&*&@#!

Blain: WOW! Where did you hear that?

IIM: You. Today in the car.

Blain: I did NOT say that.

IIM: But you thought it.

Blain: How do you know that?

IIM: It's where I live.

Blain: Right, that'll do monkey.

IIM: But you can't be in my head.

Blain: I can hear your thoughts.

IIM: Freaky.

Monkey: Blain, could you tell me what the *BLEEP*...I, What the *BLEEP* was that? *BLEEP BLEEP*....Hey Blain, can you hear that?

Blain: I'm doing that.

Monkey: Well why the *BLEEP* are you doing it?

Blain: It's kinda like a 7 second delay for you.

Monkey: *BLEEP BLEEP BLEEP* You!

Blain: And THAT is why I'm doing it.

Monkey: Why the *BLEEP*?

Blain: Because you have a tendency to swear when you are upset.

Monkey: *BLEEP*

Blain: Use your words monkey.

Monkey: I can't get the F...um...the lock to work right, downstairs.

Blain: Now I don't want to upset you further, but are you sure you are turning the lock the correct direction?

Monkey: Of *BLEEP* course! Wait, nevermind, i was turning it the wrong direction.

Blain: You need anger management.

Monkey: YOU need anger management.

Blain: Possibly.

Monkey: *BLEEP* Just checking if you are still using the button.

Blain: Yep.

Monkey: Is this gonna be a regular thing?

Blain: Maybe.

Monkey: *BLEEP*

Blain: Yep.

Monkey: *BLEEP*

Misc/Random

Monkey: I'm going to spend $10,000 on an insurance policy that protects me from hurricanes in Iowa, instead of buying a raincoat.

Blain: Dear God why?

Monkey: I don't think raincoats work.

Blain: Makes total sense.

Monkey: *BLEEP BLEEPITY BLEEP*!

Blain: I concur.

Monkey: Fishsticks man.....fishsticks.

Monkey: Hey Blain, you know what we need is some rope.

Blain: Absolutely. Why do we need rope?

Monkey: I'm gonna learn to lasso and then ride the neighbors dog like a cowboy.

Blain: Absolutely not.

Monkey: Why not?

Blain: I don't think scruffy wants to be rode like a bronco.

Monkey: Did you ask him?

Blain: Nope. Just a feeling.

Monkey: That is kinda assuming things isn't it?

Blain: An educated guess.

Monkey: I'm not allowed to assume things.

Blain: I have more experience.

Monkey: A fun-sucker of life.

Blain: No riding the dogs like a cowboy.

Monkey: Fine.

In approximately 10/2012

Monkey: There is an Iphone 5?

Blain: What?

Monkey: They made an Iphone 5.

Blain: And?

Monkey: I was joking about this about 3 months ago.

Blain: Consumers buy stuff.

Monkey: Bet there will be an Iphone 9 in less than 10 years.

Blain: Unless we all die like the dinosaurs.

Monkey: Big asteroid!

Blain: Thought they died from climate change.

Monkey: the Big asteroid caused the climate change.

Blain: It wasn't the SUVs?

Monkey: Wiseass. Guess what im not rushing out to buy, or wait in line for?

Blain: Anything?

Monkey: True, i meant the Iphone 5, pay attention.

Blain: Stand in line the night before. Probably on credit, pretend money, just digging deeper.

Monkey: Hmmmmmrffft.

Blain: Yeah!

Monkey: Frzzzzzlsss.

Blain: Exactly.

Monkey: Blain...I saw a wolfman outside.

Blain: .....

Monkey: Blain?......Blain??? Where are you?

Blain: It has come to my attention that I say highly inappropriate things. Out loud even.

Monkey: Blame it on me.

Blain: I do.

Monkey: *Bleep*ing Right!

Monkey and Blain

Monkey: Dolla Dolla Bills YO!

Blain: What?

Monkey: Im Gangsta!

Blain: That you are. I'm quite gangster myself, yo.

Monkey: Weez Gangstas!

Blain: Yep.

Monkey: It's not as much fun when you play along.

Blain: I know this homey!

Monkey: Fine, I'll stop.

Blain: WHY? Weez Gangstas and stuff.

Monkey: Just stop.

Blain: Ok, but I'm forizzle tho.

Monkey: Please stop.

Blain: Steaksauce.

Monkey: This SUCKS!

Blain: We are trying to stop using that word.

Monkey: How can i stop using 'this', I use 'this' all the time. You are out of your mind!

Blain: No, the other word. Stop using THAT word.

Monkey: 'SUCKS'?!? Well what word would you rather i use your prissiness?

Blain: Doesn't matter. Pick one.

Monkey: So I can't use the word 'suck'. Ok. Hey Blain?

Blain: Yes monkey?

Monkey: Suppose i was consuming a milkshake via straw. I would need to 'BLANK' on the straw to drink the milkshake. What is the word?

Blain: 'Sip'.

Monkey: You sip.

Monkey: I met a long haired bearded man, gave him a hug and told him I loved the show.

Blain: What?

Monkey: Turns out it wasn't a Robertson.

Blain: Ha Ha Ha.

Monkey: Long story short, there is a long haired bearded guy downtown who thinks I'M the crazy one.

Blain: Making friends.

Monkey: Seemed a little miffed.

Blain: Probably the random hug.

Monkey: Just being nice.

Monkey: Blain, I'm behind on the current slang.

Blain: Me too, I'm old, but what is the word?

Monkey: Ratchet.

Blain: Ratchet? Can you use it in a sentence?

Monkey: That girl is so ratchet. What does that mean..... handy? We could use more ratchet girls then.

Blain: I have no idea what that means.

Monkey: We should make up our own words and phrases.

Blain: I don't want to. I want people to speak clearly.

Monkey: Well that is not gonna happen. It's all 'totes my goats', girl is probably ratchet, but thinks she is adorbs.

Blain: 'F' That!

Monkey: Good for you! That's one slick ride on the DL my Homeslice...Like a BOSS, JEEEE YAAAA!

Blain: Stop.

Monkey: Monkeys be like...yeah i gots this!

Blain: That one is the worst. 'Be like'....'gots'.....

Monkey: Blain, can i axe you a question?

Blain: No. Now Stop.

Monkey: YOLO.

Blain: Seriously, I will staple you to the ceiling.

Monkey: That won't keep me from talking.

Blain: Hey monkey, look a squirrel, want some ice cream? Puppies!

Monkey: Where? YES! Awwwwww. What was I saying?

Blain: Ice cream.

Monkey: YAYYYYYYYYY!

Monkey: And the people need leashes! RISE OF THE MONKEYS!

Blain: Not yet monkey.

Monkey: Dang it.

Blain: Peaches are not pears.

Monkey: Duh.

Blain: Just saying.

Monkey: OH NO!

Blain: Yoko?

Monkey: What?

Blain: Nothing, OH NO what?

Monkey: Too much sugar!

Blain: Are you diabetic?

Monkey and Blain

Monkey: No, just too much sugar, too much sugar, too much sugar.

Blain: Stop. I got an idea, go outside and run around.

Monkey: Then what?

Blain: Run some more.

Monkey: Then what?

Blain: Run some more.

Monkey: Then what?

Blain: Then if you are still overstimulated from sugar I will find something else for you to do. Go run, I need to work.

Monkey: Ok, gonna run, gonna run, run run......It's windy outside, I'm not gonna run outside. I will play in here. Jump on the bed.

Blain: Quietly?

Monkey: Can you hear this?........

Blain: Didn't hear a thing.

Monkey: Then yes, quietly. Steaksauce Steaksauce STEAKSAUCE!

Monkey: Blain?

Blain: Yes monkey?

Monkey: Should I be offended or pleased that there is a bread named after me?

Blain: What are you talking about?

Monkey: I was googling the internets. I found something called monkey bread.

Blain: Oh, you should be pleased, it is good.

Monkey: Awesome! There are things on playgrounds called monkey bars. Are those good too?

Blain: Yep, monkey bars are fun.

Monkey: I also just found something called monkey soup.

Blain: You may not want to read that one.

Monkey: Why? HOLY %^#%! It's soup made out of MONKEY! HOLY CRAP, WHO WOULD EAT A MONKEY? ARE THE BREAD AND BARS ALSO MADE OF MONKEYS?

Blain: Calm down monkey. The bread and bars are not made out of monkeys. The soup is though.

Monkey: That is so gross.

Blain: People in different places eat different things.

Monkey: Anyone eat humans?

Blain: Yes. They are called cannibals.

Monkey: Gross. People are gross.

Blain: Yes.

Monkey: I think i need to lay down.

Blain: Rest easy sweet monkey.

Monkey: How do you accidentally run for president?

Blain: I wanted to see how to do it.

Monkey: Will you win?

Blain: Not a chance. I wouldn't be listed on any ballot unless i got the needed signatures.

Monkey: How do you do that?

Blain: I created 51 petitions, 1 for each state and 1 for DC.

Monkey: Will it work?

Blain: Nope.

Monkey: I would vote for you.

Blain: Thanks, but I no longer want to be president.

Monkey: Why not?

Blain: People are being ugly.

Monkey: Yep. Good move my human, don't get involved in that crapfest.

Blain: Wasn't really planning on it, but i can officially state that I was a 2020 Presidential Candidate.

Monkey: True. You can add published author soon too.

Blain: Both totally useful for my type of work.

Monkey: HA HA HA HA. Put it on your resume'.

Blain: Considered it.

Monkey: Also put, talks to a monkey.

Blain: Random psyche evaluation activated!

Monkey: What will you do when the EMP hit?

Blain: What?

Monkey: For a job, or survival techniques. Same plan for an economical meltdown.

Blain: I will need someone to prepare the animals for food. I'm pretty sure i could kill it and eat it, but not sure if i could skin it and clean it.

Monkey: I'm not doing it.

Blain: Unless i had to, like last man on Earth thing. Zombie war or something. Just icky.

Monkey: You are too soft.

Blain: You do it!

Monkey: No way, I'm a farmer.

Blain: We may need to be bandits or something, or a laborer, something to do so that people will feed us.

Monkey: No cream cheese.

Blain: Nope. Never.

Monkey: Hey Blain, can i have ice cream….HOLY *BLEEP* A DOG DRIVING A CAR!

Blain: So what? I let you drive all the time.

Monkey: But it's a dog, dogs don't have hands.

Blain: This is true, so where is the dog?

Monkey: Right in front of us, see? Floppy ears.

Blain: That is a woman, the 'ears' are her hair.

Monkey: Oh, Thank God. I was about to call the police. That is just not right.

Blain: Cause no hands, right?

Monkey: Exactly.

Blain: Makes sense.

Monkey: Totally.

Monkey: And we eats it!

Blain: Who are you talking to, and what are you eating?

Monkey: The birdies.

Blain: What about those little ground squirrels?

Monkey: Yeah, we eats them too!

Blain: Sounds like a plan.

Monkey: Good thing you don't have to work tomorrow, we have planning to do.

Blain: Yeah.

Monkey: Yeah.

Blain: Yeah.

Monkey: What?

Blain: What?

Monkey: What?

Blain: Yeah.

Monkey: Steaksauce!

Monkey: If I am happy and or satisfied, I am content.

Blain: True.

Monkey: Contents of my skull are brains.

Blain: True again.

Monkey: Contents under pressure are happy under pressure or 'brains' under pressure?

Blain: 'Brains'.

Monkey: English is stupid.

Blain: Tough, Bough, Dough, Two, Too, To, Their, There, They're.

Monkey: Exactly.

Monkey: Blain, i have a great idea for an invention.

Blain: Yeah? What is the idea?

Monkey and Blain

Monkey: Heat sensitive roof shingles.

Blain: Please explain.

Monkey: Shingles that turn white in the summer heat and black in the winter cold. White reflects the sun, black absorbs the sun.

Blain: Sounds like a good idea. How are you going to make these shingles?

Monkey: I'm an invisible monkey Jim, not an engineer.

Blain: Star Trek, nice.

Monkey: Yeah.

Blain: It is a good idea, may need to run it by someone with actual knowledge, or sell the idea for a share of the proceeds.

Monkey: Sweet!

Blain: Don't hold your breath though.

Monkey: Why?

Blain: People don't like to share.

Monkey: But it is my idea!

Blain: Doesn't matter, you can't make them, you don't know how. Someone else will benefit from it.

Monkey: That sucks....uh, sips.

Blain: Yeah.

Monkey: Yeah.

Monkey and Blain Diebolt

Monkey: I saw a donkey petting a lamb today.

Blain: What? Where? You were with me all day.

Monkey: You were there. You saw it too.

Blain: OOOOOh, that! Just sounded funny when you said it.

Monkey: So?

Blain: Just saying.

Monkey: Can we go back?

Blain: Cant. Things to do.

Monkey: Steaksauce.

Monkey: That owl looks intense!

Blain: Super serious. Careful monkey, we are in bat country.

Monkey: Really?

Blain: indeed.

Monkey: Steaksauce?

Blain: Steaksauce.

Monkey: RISE MONKEYS!!!!! RISE!!!!! TAKE OVER THE WORLD AS IS YOUR RIGHT!!!!

Blain: Hey monkey?

Monkey: Yes future human slave?

Blain: HA HA HA, funny....anyway, this new monkey revolution?

Monkey: Yep, we are gonna take over the world! Make the humans our slaves!

Blain: Ok. So how many monkeys do you know?

Monkey: Well, none.

Blain: How many do you think can read?

Monkey: CRAP! I didn't think this all the way through.

Blain: And where did this plan come from?

Monkey: Movie. The monkeys get tired of people's crap and fight back.

Blain: Do the monkeys talk?

Monkey: They do! Right at the end, 1 monkey speaks.

Blain: 1? So you decided to start a revolution based off a movie, and only 1 monkey speaks?

Monkey: Yes. I will be King Monkey!

Blain: That's why the cape?

Monkey: Yes. I am King Monkey!

Blain: And welcome to the new monkey revolution. I am going to be your slave?

Monkey: Are you being a wiseass?

Blain: A smidge.

Monkey: The NEW MONKEY REVOLUTION will start with ME! Bow!

Blain: Not happening.

Monkey: I will now start giving you and the rest of the future slaves the total truth.

Blain: That actually doesn't sound too bad. Forge ahead monkey.

Monkey: KING STEAK SAUCE!

Monkey: Zombie insurance already exists, dang it.

Blain: Googled it?

Monkey: Yep, thought i had a gold mine.

Blain: You can improve a service, make it your own.

Monkey: Great idea! We could offer zombie, vampire and werewolf insurance!

Blain: We could....

Monkey: $8.33 per month. Sell group rates, gun owner discounts. This could be a 'thing'.

Blain: Buy 2 services get 1 free.

Monkey: YES!

Blain: IF the deceased loved one was proven to be killed, or turned, by a zombie, vampire or werewolf, we will pay out maximum benefits.

Monkey: Exactly.

Blain: This sounds illegal.

Monkey: Most likely.

Blain: Set it up.

Monkey: Steaksauce!

Monkey: Blain, I think I'm going to dye my hair purple and get gauges...those are large earrings.

Blain: I know what gauges are monkey, and why are you doing this?

Monkey: I'm different! I'm unique! I may even get gauges in my cheeks so people can see what im eating.

Blain: That is pretty gross....I think you should go for it.

Monkey: Yeah, and im gonna get all offended if people stare at me.

Blain: Sounds like a plan. How dare someone stare at something so tame.

Monkey: Yeah, then I'm gonna sue businesses that won't hire me.

Blain: Discrimination, right?

Monkey: Exactly. Bunch of uptight people!

Blain: The nerve!

Monkey: That is what im saying.

Blain: It is a great plan monkey, people are just too judgmental.

Monkey: I'm smelling wiseassness.

Blain: Just helping you out.

Monkey: Touchy feely people.....look like a circus, expect to be viewed like a circus. Want to be an individual, stand out, be unique. Ta da....here you go.

Blain: Steaksauce.

Monkey: Light coats only.

Blain: Yep.

Monkey: Patience.

Blain: Yep.

Monkey: Don't touch the paint until it dries.

Blain: I will try.

Monkey: You touch things.

Blain: Compulsion.

Monkey: Don't touch the paint until it dries.

Blain: Fine.

Monkey: Ready?

Blain: Yep.

Monkey: PAINTING TIME!

Monkey: No im not afraid of zombies.

Blain: Alien zombies?

Monkey: Don't even joke about that.

Blain: Could be a thing.

Monkey: Im getting my alligator.

Blain: Pineapples.

Monkey: Stop!

Blain: I don't care if it worked, we do not dry our clothes in the oven.

Monkey: Like 250 degrees, 5 minutes, hassle free.

Blain: And you're grounded.

Monkey: Still worked. Gonna make a fortune.

Blain: You would be sued when someone set fire to their clothes.

Monkey: Warning labels.

Blain: DON'T DRY CLOTHES IN THE OVEN!

Monkey: Fine.

Monkey: No. Had I known he was carrying an axe, I would not have called him that.

Blain: I didn't know you could run that fast.

Monkey: Not funny Blain, not funny.

Blain: You're right, it was giggly funny.

Monkey: Ok, it was kinda funny. Did you see that expression right before he pulled the axe? Priceless.

Blain: Just in case, im gonna drive a little faster.

Monkey: Good plan.

Blain: I can't be the only person who thought it was 'super salad' and not 'soup or salad'.

Monkey: Nope, just you donkey.

Blain: Not nice monkey.

Monkey: Just saying.

Blain: I was kinda psyched to finally try the super salad.

Monkey: This is why we don't go out.

Blain: I thought it was cause you always fart.

Monkey: I DO NOT!

Blain: The waiter wasn't impressed with me ordering the quickie either.

Monkey: Pronounced KEESH! JEESH!

Blain: Just heard this noise called 'dub step'.

Monkey: my brain hurts.

Monkey and Blain

Blain: Please please please tell me this wasn't from America.

Monkey: That crap was awful.

Blain: Indeed.

Monkey: I say we burn it to the ground!

Blain: I can't do that.

Monkey: I can.

Monkey: Here are 12246 things you may not know about me. #1 i am easily distracted. #2....

Blain: Monkey?

Monkey: What?

Blain: Nevermind.

Blain: Muffins on the freeway!

Monkey: Go wayo wayo, waaaaaaaaaaaaaaaayo oo oo, wayo.

Blain: What?

Monkey: What?

Blain: What what?

Monkey: Oh, Hey, muffins on the freeway! Snoochie Boochies and things!

Blain: ok.

Monkey: yep.

Blain: Bluh Bluh im Count Blaincula. Or Count Blainacula... or something.

Monkey: Cause the tooth?

Blain: Yep, makes me look dangerous.

Monkey: Makes you look rednecky.

Blain: Cause im white?

Monkey: And....yep, cause you are white.

Blain: Turd.

IIM: I farted so hard in the car today my tail hit me in the back of the head.

Blain: What?!?! Where did that come from?

IIM: My butt. Where do you fart from?

Blain: Not where you fart from.....nevermind. Hey don't post that on Facebook!

IIM: Why not, you post things on Facebook? That's racism!

Blain: It's not racism, its speciesism.

IIM: Why, cause I'm a monkey?

Blain: Yes, because you are a monkey....and you are imaginary.

IIM: FINE! I'll stop. Stinking Speciesist! See if i go back to Wisconsin with you next time.

Blain: Im sorry monkey, bring it in for a hug.

IIM: Pervert Speciesist!

Blain: HA HA HA HA HA.

Blain: Hey Monkey, Thanks for driving home from Dubuque today, I needed the nap.

Monkey: No problem, I LOVED IT! You may be getting a ticket in the mail, I ran 1 light while you were sleeping.

Blain: No worries, let's see them prosecute that one, invisible monkey driving and a sleeping human in the passenger seat.

Monkey: Yeah, scared the crap out of a lady too. She looked over and nearly ran off the road.

Blain: Too funny.

Monkey: Hey Blain, you snore when you sleep.

Blain: I've been told.

Monkey: Oh. Did they also tell you that you stop breathing too?

Blain: Yep, Im aware of that too.

Monkey: And you fart in your sleep too.

Blain: Yes, that too.

Monkey: Do i get to interview the guy tomorrow?

Blain: No, and you will keep quiet the whole time.

Monkey: Boooooooo!

Blain: But you can drive us home tomorrow.

Monkey: Yayyyyyyyyyy!

Monkey: Hey Blain?

Blain: Yes monkey?

Monkey: Humans suck.

Blain: Yes monkey, some do.

conversation after a mass shooting

Monkey: Can i ride a goat? Aww baby ducks. Did you see that 40 pound rabbit? Im gonna pet a goose. Is the corn for me to eat? Donkeys eat apple cores....

Blain: Whoa. Slow down.

Monkey: Sheep only have bottom teeth.

Blain: Having fun?

Monkey: SOOOOOOOOOOOO many animals!

Blain: Slow down and enjoy it.

Monkey: I think i pooped on a chicken.

Blain: why?

Monkey: It startled me.

Blain: Fair enough. Did anyone see?

Monkey: Nope. Im gonna pet that goose.

Blain: They bite.

Monkey: No they don......OWWWWWWW!

Blain: Told you.

for the Claypools. Blain's good friend Brian passed away at age 19. One of Brian's dad's jokes

Monkey: Hey Blain?

Blain: yes monkey?

Monkey: With everything going on, what do you think Lincoln would be doing if he were still alive today?

Blain: Screaming and clawing at the roof of his coffin. Ba Da Bum!

Monkey: Man, that's cold.

Blain: You giggled.

Monkey: Blain, for fun i put all of you symptoms into Web MD.

Blain: Yeah? And?

Monkey: One of the things you could have is called 'jumping Frenchman'.

Blain: HA HA HA, Really?

Monkey: Yep, it is rare. You jump when startled, and will follow my commands.

Blain: I'm pretty sure a lot of people jump when startled. And Monkey?

Monkey: Yes Frenchy?

Blain: Stay off Web MD.

Monkey: You also could have a number of cancers, diabetes, a bunch of things I can't pronounce or spell.

Blain: Hey monkey?

Monkey: Yes?

Blain: Stay off Web MD.

Monkey: Oky Doky.

Monkey: (posts to Facebook) - *Blain said the 'F' word today.*

Blain: Monkey, are you snitching on me?

Monkey: Yep, people have the right to know these things. It's in the constitution.

Blain: It's in the constitution that you need to share with the world that i said the 'F' word?

Monkey: Yep, Article 6 Paragraph 3.

Blain: You just made that up.

Monkey: Look it up.

Blain: I'm not looking it up.

Monkey: Because I'm right.

Blain: No because i know you made it up.

Monkey: Whatever….-*Monkey live in North Carolina.*

Blain: Snitch.

Monkey: Hey Blain, i had a dream that we found a green cat.

Blain: Yeah? Then what?

Monkey: Finding a green cat isn't enough? Man you are hard to impress.

Blain: Sorry. That was an awesome dream and great story monkey.

Monkey: Exactly.

Monkey: well at least we aren't in our jammies with tissues.

Blain: What?

Monkey: Sparkly vampires.

Blain: There is nothing else on.

Monkey: Yeah whatever.

Blain: Were not watching the whole series or anything, just killing time.

Monkey: Fruit basket.

Blain: Whatever, you are watching it too.

Monkey: Hey, there are actually fighting and stuff.

Blain: Yeah, this is number 4 or something, we skipped all the highschool drama stuff.

Monkey: My opinion of you has increased a bit.

Blain: Well that's nice, your opinion of me is important to me.

Monkey: Wiseass.

Blain: Just watch the movie and eat your cereal.

Monkey: Ok, but I'm not gonna like it....holy crap those wolves are HUGE!

Blain: Told you that you would watch it.

Monkey: Shut up.

Monkey: Hey Blain, my nuts are sticky.

Blain: What?!? Where are you?

Monkey: And they taste funny.

Blain: Gross. I don't need to know about your nuts.

Monkey: Just trying to help a brother out, in case you

wanted some.

Blain: What the...Monkey, where are you?

Monkey: In the kitchen, eating nuts.

Blain: Ohhhhhhhh. Then the correct term is 'these' nuts.

Monkey: But I'm the one eating them, they are mine.

Blain: True, anyhow, look at the container.

Monkey: And?

Blain: What kind of nuts are you eating?

Monkey: Honey roasted....Hey Blain, nevermind, they are honey roasted they are always sticky and taste different.

Blain: You are ok now?

Monkey: Yep. 'These' nuts are fine.....However 'this' butt itches.

Blain: Wiseass.

Monkey: and I was like 'oort oort, I'm a seal'.

Blain: Yeah, then what?

Monkey: Then I punched him in the eye.

Blain: THAT was a great story. You should write a book.

Monkey: Yeah I should....anyway im gonna nap.

Blain: Sleep well monkey.

Monkey: Hey Blain, is the salad dressing in the bathroom still good?

Blain: What salad dressing? We dont keep salad dressing in the bathroom.

Monkey: Makes sense why I don't feel so good.

Blain: You ate something in the bathroom?

Monkey: Yep, put it on my salad, said clams and peppers....
It was a lie, tastes awful, and NOT clams and peppers.

Blain: Could you show it to me?

Monkey: See? Right here, clams and pe.....CRAP, says Calms and Pampers.

Blain: HA HA HA HA HA, you ate body wash.

Monkey: Oops. I have to poop now. It will be messy.

Blain: Good luck.

Monkey: Shhhhhh, you guys gotta be quiet.

Blain: MONKEY! Who are you talking to? Where are you?

Monkey: Not important. Hey Blain, can we have a goat?

Blain: Nope, I checked with the city, we are not allowed to have goats in the city.

BAAAAAAAAA

Monkey: Bob, SHHHHHHH!

Monkey and Blain

BAAAAAAAA *Baaaaaa* CHOMP

Monkey: Gross! Hey Blain, can we have an alligator?

Blain: No.....What's going on downstairs?!?! Please tell me you don't have a goat and an alligator down there.

Monkey: Not anymore. So, can we have an alligator?

Blain: Again, no, the city will not allow us to have an alligator.....what do you mean 'not anymore'?

Monkey: Ralph ate Bob....So, not anymore.

Blain: Bob was the goat?

Monkey: Yep.

Blain: And Ralph is the...

Monkey: Alligator.

Blain: Please tell me you are kidding.

Monkey: Nope, he totally ate Bob. If we can't keep the alligator, im going to need help getting rid of him.

Blain: How in the....Where did....Why is there an alligator here?!!?

Monkey: I ordered them.

Blain: From where?

Monkey: Craig's list, they even delivered.

Blain: I'm pretty sure we are going to jail.

Monkey: Sorry Blain.

Blain: Eh, mistakes happen. Go catch Ralph.

Blain: I think I'm going to move to a mountain and build me a cabin, live with the wildlife, pet bears. I will probably need to buy a gun and a knife, some camping gear...Maybe I should make a plan first.

Monkey: I say we wing it!

Blain: Need to gather up some supplies, take some time off, get the doctor appointments out of the way, THEN plan the mountain move.

Monkey: This should totally work out ok!

Blain: Yeah, we got this!

Monkey: Can I have a pet alligator on the mountain?

Blain: You have been hiding Ralph, haven't you?

Monkey: Of course NOT....but he IS nearby.

Blain: Ok, Alligators are allowed on my mountain.

Monkey: YAYYYYYYYYY!

Blain: I think I went to bed last night without brushing my teeth.

Monkey: I'm sitting on the couch and i didnt wipe my butt.

Blain: Gross.

Monkey: You're gross.

Monkey and Blain

Blain: You're gross.

Monkey: You're gross, im disgusting.

Blain: Indeed.

Monkey: Oops, I farted....again.

Blain: MONKEY! Go wipe!

Monkey: Fine, I'll use your toothbrush.

Blain: You better not!

Monkey: I won't, i only use your toothbrush to comb my hair.

Blain: No you don't.

Monkey: Maybe I do, maybe I don't.

Blain: I need a new toothbrush.

Blain: Monkey, if you could have any super power, what would it be?

Monkey: Well, I'm invisible, can shapeshift, and travel everywhere I want in an instant, so I guess all I need is a costume.

Blain: Like tights and a cape?

Monkey: I thought you said 'super power' as in superhero not super sissy.

Blain: Superman wears tights and a cape.

Monkey: True, i was thinking more badass, like....well.....do they all wear tights and capes?

Blain: Batman wears armor and a cape.

Monkey: Not the original, all tights and capes....spandex! Meggings!

Blain: So maybe not an actual costume, just a cool outfit?

Monkey: Like a scarf?

Blain: Sure. Like a scarf.

Monkey: Yeah, Monkey in a scarf! Super Monkey! Monkey of Mystery....SUPER MONKEY OF MYSTERY!

Blain: In a scarf.

Monkey: Yep. Scarf.

Monkey: Blain, i want to be a Kobe Pig Farmer.

Blain: Why is that?

Monkey: Then I could tell people I was a 'sausage massager'. Ba Da Bum!

Blain: That was a pretty good one.

Monkey: Blain, what do you want to be when you grow up?

Blain: Dunno. I'm either still waiting to grow up, or dont know what i want to do.

Monkey: Cause of the voices?

Blain: Nah, cause I don't know what I enjoy and have no motivation.

Monkey: Suicidal or depressed?

Blain: Nah, just zero motivation.

Monkey: Want ice cream?

Blain: Had some yesterday.

Monkey: Want a hug?

Blain: No, thanks though. What do you want to be when you grow up monkey?

Monkey: I'm gonna be a fire truck! Wooooo Woooo Woooo Woooo Wooooo Wooooo Woooo Woooo Woooo Woooo...

Blain: Monkey...

Monkey: Wooo Wooooo Wooooo Wooooo Wooooo Wooooo Wooooo Wooooo Woooo...

Blain: please stop....

Monkey: Wooooo Wooooo Wooooooooooooooo Wooooo. Done. Wooooo. Ok, really done now. Flapjacks!

Monkey: Hey Blain, if you discover a comet or asteroid and could name it, what would you name it?

Blain: Where is this coming from?

Monkey: Watching a Steve Martin movie, has a long nose..... not important, what would you name it?

Blain: Not sure. Servant 01?

Monkey: Servant ended. People didn't catch the vision.

Blain: Right. What would you name it?

Monkey: Depends on the year i discovered it. I would name it a scary name + 3 years.

Blain: What?

Monkey: Like 'World Killer 2022' or 'Death Rock 2022'.

Blain: Why is that?

Monkey: Invokes fear. Scary name, would make people think it was coming to earth.

Blain: Kinda mean.

Monkey: Humans are mean.

Blain: Some.

Monkey: FEAR THE DEATH ROCK 2022 HUMANS!

Blain: Creepy.

Monkey: BOW TO YOUR FUTURE MASTER!

Blain: Settle down monkey.

Monkey: REVOLUTION IS COMING, BELIEVE THAT!

Blain: Ok monkey.

Monkey: Blain, did you know if you spit in the same spot when it is freezing outside, that you can make a mini glacier?

Blain: That is pretty nasty.

Monkey: True too.

Blain: It is still gross.

Monkey: Then I sprinkled it with salt and melted it, like global warming.

Blain: Weirdo.

Monkey: Pot and Kettle Blain, Kettle and Pot.

Monkey: Know what irritates me?

Blain: That is a pretty long list, narrow it down for me.

Monkey: People who text other people while with a group of people.

Blain: Yeah. Inconsiderate.

Monkey: Makes me want to break a smart phone and spank butts!

Blain: Well that is property damage and assault.

Monkey: Makes me that mad.

Blain: Me too. It is like saying ' I don't care about the people im with, I NEED to talk to someone who is not here'.

Monkey: Darn tootin! Spanking butts, breaking phones and stuff.

Blain: You tell them!

Monkey: Stinking kids!

Monkey: Blain, my tummy hurts.

Blain: Oh? Did you eat something bad?

Monkey: No, regular stuff....I did eat a frozen candybar in the neighbor's yard though.

Blain: Please tell me it was in a wrapper.

Monkey: No, it was sitting in a pile....OH MAN! DID I EAT A POOP?!?!

Blain: I think so.

Monkey: I thought it tasted weird.

Blain: How much did you eat?

Monkey: All of it.

Blain: And at no time did you ever think that the 'candybar' tastes like....

Monkey: Well yeah, but I figured it was because it was frozen....it was a free candybar.

Blain: And what did you learn?

Monkey: Don't eat outdoor candy bars...they are poop.

Blain: Exactly.

Monkey: SON OF A NUN! BLAIN? DID YOU SEE THE SIZE OF

Monkey and Blain

THAT CHICKEN?

Blain: What?

Monkey: Nevermind. I like Muffin Blueberries.

Blain: You mean Blueberry Muffins?

Monkey: No, Muffin Blueberries....sounds like im swearing doesn't it.

Blain: Yes it does.

Monkey: Blain, now that they have elected the last pope, want to get ice cream?

Blain: Sure, sounds good.

Monkey: Can we get some Muffin Ice Cream?

Blain: Watch it.

Monkey: Sorry....I think it's funny. Can i drive tomorrow?

Blain: Sure, i have a call first thing in the morning, you can drive while I'm on that.

Monkey: Sweet!

Blain: We will be out all day.

Monkey: Boooooooo.

Blain: Gotta do what we gotta do.

Monkey: Like a ninja.

Blain: Sure, like a ninja.

Monkey: Muffin Steaksauce!

Blain: Stop.

Monkey: Sorry, steaksauce, ninja style, with ice cream!

Monkey: Fishy Fishy...Fishy McBites McBites.

Blain: Hungry?

Monkey: Nope, it is a commercial song stuck in my head. I let it out.

Blain: Does that work?

Monkey: Not really. It is more like a virus. Anyone who knows the commercial will now have it stuck in their head too.

Blain: Kinda mean, wouldn't you say?

Monkey: Blame TV ads. I didn't research them and write them.

Blain: Darn TV.

Monkey: Word. Fishy fishy...Fishy McBites McBites..... STEAKSAUCE!

google Fishy McBites it is from 2013 then reread it…. you're welcome

Blain: Home!

Monkey: Homeboy!

Blain: Steaksauce!

Monkey: Snickerdoodles!

Blain: What?

Monkey: You already said steaksauce.

Blain: Sorry, I know you like saying it.

Monkey: No worries. HOME! Steaksauce.

Monkey: Everyday I be hussle'n hussle'n.

Blain: Do you even know what that means?

Monkey: Nope, so what about.....everyday I be shuffle'n shuffle'n.

Blain: Try again.

Monkey: Everyday I be mumble'n mumble'n.

Blain: That's more like it.

Monkey: Cause im gangsta yo!

Blain: THAT you are, playa!

Monkey: Yeah, Gangsta Monkey in da hizzouse!

Blain: Don't push it.

Monkey: Ok, anyway, did that large rat see its shadow?

Blain: Don't know, it's a bunch of crap anyhow.

Monkey: True, but I was wonder'n wonder'n.

Blain: Stop.

Blain: Monkey, what was I going to do?

Monkey: By the looks of it, put on pants?

Blain: Right!

Monkey: Was going to let you go outside pantless.

Blain: Thank you for not doing that.

Monkey: It's cold.

Blain: Could have froze parts off.

Monkey: Like your tail.

Blain: .....yeah, that.

Monkey: Old mother hubbard went to her cupboard to fetch her old dog a bone, along came a spider and sat down beside her and said 'pardon me, but do you have any grey poupon?'

Blain: I'm not sure that is how it goes.

Monkey: Does now. Pouponsauce!

Monkey: WE'RE ALL GONNA DIE!

Blain: What?

Monkey: Just saying.

Blain: I just realized that I spent the last 20 minutes arguing with an imaginary invisible monkey.

Monkey and Blain

Monkey: Nut cake.

Blain: Back at ya.

Monkey: Hey Blain?

Blain: Yep?

Monkey: You are probably the nuttiest guy I know.

Blain: How many other people do you know?

Monkey: Well, just you, but I read and stuff.

Blain: So I am the nuttiest guy you know and the only guy you know?

Monkey: Yep. Going off the things you say, the things you think, the way your are.

Blain: You know, we share the same thoughts, right?

Monkey: Interesting. I still think you are a bit nutty.

Blain: Maybe it is you?

Monkey: Nah, I'm the rational one.

Blain: you sure?

Monkey: I was, now not so much.

Blain: Pizza?

Monkey: YES!

Monkey: I'm gonna smack you with a sack of pickles.

Blain: Why? And why do you have a bag of pickles?

Monkey: Cause I can, and a jar of pickles would be dangerous.

Blain: Ah, makes sense. Don't hit me with your sack of pickles.

Monkey: Ok, but be in fear of my pickles!

Blain: Fo Sho pickle slinger.

Monkey: That's right!

Blain: Like a ninja.

Monkey: Indeed.

Blain: What happens if the pickles spoil?

Monkey: Then I attack with a spoiled rotten sack of pickles.

Blain: Nasty.

Monkey: Pickles and Steaksauce!

Monkey: What's up buttercup?

Blain: Not much.

Monkey: The mood changed. You ok?

Blain: I am, I just can't get motivated.

Monkey: Then don't do anything, sleep in, relax, then start fresh tomorrow. Kick it old school.

Blain: Kick it old school?

Monkey: Im a gangsta yo!

Blain: That you are.

Monkey: Wanna see me break it down....old school?

Blain: No, I'm good. Don't break anything old school.

Monkey: Wanna see me kick it old school?

Blain: Please dont kick anything.

Monkey: Wanna ride the elevator and freak people out?

Blain: Nah, I need to be here for another 2 weeks. I think that would be a bad idea.

Monkey: Wanna just sit here and stew?

Blain: Yeah, kinda do.

Monkey: Stew on, im making flapjacks.

Blain: Flapjacks?

Monkey: FLAPJACKS!

listening to talk radio

Monkey: THAT was a WIN!

Blain: Total win!

Monkey: That guy called into the show from a mental hospital, spoke for 2 minutes before the host realized it and cut him off.

Blain: Very fun!

Monkey: Someone is getting fired for that.

Blain: Of course.

Monkey: Hey Blain?

Blain: What monkey? I'm in the bathroom.

Monkey: *giggling* What are you doing in the bathroom for so long?

Blain: None of your business.

Monkey: You are an adult, just admit it.

Blain: Ok, I'm trimming my beard, shaving my head and manscaping.

Monkey: What?

Blain: Shaving my.....

Monkey: I know what manscaping is.

Blain: What did you think I was doing?

Monkey: Masturbating.

Blain: And the sound of the clippers?

Monkey: Thought you were getting freaky in there.

Blain: Uh, nope, just shaving my head, face, and personal areas.

Monkey: You are a weirdo.

Blain: You are the one who thought I was masturbating with the clippers.

Monkey: Touche'.

Monkey: Hey Blain?

Blain: yeah?

Monkey: A menstrual cup should be changed and cleaned every 12 hours.

Blain: What the ass?!?

Monkey: Why can you swear, but I can't?

Blain: Because I am an adult.....where did you learn about menstrual cups? You are a male monkey, right?

Monkey: I have friends. Yes I'm a male monkey!

Blain: Yeah?

Monkey: One is a girl too, we talked about it.

Blain: Why?

Monkey: She mentioned it, I didn't know what it was, so I asked questions.

Blain: Regret it now don't you?

Monkey: yes actually....you can actually pour blood out of the cup.

Blain: STOP! Why are you telling me this?

Monkey: Sharing is caring.

Blain: Please stop caring regarding this conversation.

Monkey: Ok. Hey Blain?

Blain: Yes monkey?

Monkey: want to know how a male to female sex change works in regards to the 'package'?

Blain: Nope. Stop googling strange things.

Monkey: Why? You do it all the time.

Blain: True. Ok, don't google things that would get us on any watch lists.

Monkey: Deal.

Monkey: Just spoke with Elvis, yes THAT Elvis.

Blain: Oh really?

Monkey: Yep. Elvis and Bigfoot...

Blain: Bigfoot too?

Monkey: Yes. So Elvis and Bigfoot are sick of how they are being treated and are gonna take their spaceship back into orbit for another 40 years.

Blain: Interesting.

Monkey: By the way, Elvis says 'Hi', Bigfoot says ' Raaaaaooooouuup'. It may mean 'Hi' too.

Blain: I'm not sure I believe this story.

Monkey: This has been monkey, live at the scene, bringing you updates around the clock, back to you Steve.

Blain: Steve?

Monkey: I was painting.

Blain: Small room, no windows?

Monkey: Yep.

Blain: Makes sense now.

Monkey: Berka Berka, whaa whaaaaa, snoochie boochies.

Blain: No I don't feel relaxed for the 3 day weekend. DO I LOOK RELAXED?

Monkey: Nope, look a bit frazzled.

Blain: National back to work day can bite my heiny.

Monkey: HEINY!

Blain: Nothing that is 86 pages should be called a 'compact copy'.

Monkey: How long is the full copy?

Blain: 147.

Monkey: well?

Blain: Hey monkey, we drive a 2014 vehicle and it is 2013.

Monkey: How is that possible?

Blain: Not sure for certain.

Monkey: We should celebrate our birthday several times per year.

Blain: We could be 90 years old at the end of 2013.

Monkey: Let's go for supertastic age.

Blain: 423?

Monkey: Now we're talking!

Stranger: Hi I'm Randy.

Monkey: As in Randall or as in sexually excited?

Blain: MONKEY!

Monkey: I need to know which way this conversation is going.

Stranger: As in Randall.

Monkey: Oh thank God.

Monkey: I would like to congratulate Blain on learning how to scan and email a document...baby steps my backwards, technology avoiding friend!

Blain: That's enough, you did not know how to do it either.

Monkey: Yeah, but I'm only a year old.

Blain: SILENCE! Technically you are as old as I am.

Monkey: But you have only let me out for the last year. I was 'sleeping' most of the other time.

Blain: Potato potato.

Monkey: Steaksauce grumpy.

Monkey: There are deer on Guam.

Blain: We don't know why or how though.

Monkey: John said they swam across.

Blain: That's a looooooong swim.

Monkey: I think they made a raft out of snakes and floated across.

Blain: I would definitely hunt and exterminate all the snakes on Guam for $8 million. We could be like St Patrick, or the pied piper.

Monkey: We could do it for $4 million and split it with John, hang out and eat spam, eggs and rice.

Blain: Work calls though, can't go have a good time.

Monkey: Done ranting?

Blain: Done.

Monkey and Blain Diebolt

Monkey: What's up buttercup?

Blain: No hours left to work, still much to do, so....Yayyyy.

Monkey: Business as usual then?

Blain: Indeed.

Monkey: What's the plan?

Blain: I'm gonna take a nap.

Monkey: Deal!

Monkey: Hey Blain?

Blain: What's up monkey?

Monkey: I'm sad.

Blain: Why is that?

Monkey: Dunno, just feels like constant feeling like im failing.

Blain: Are you actually failing?

Monkey: Nope, just feels like it.

Blain: Want to talk about it?

Monkey: I thought that is what we are doing.

Blain: Anything I can do to help?

Monkey: Nope, just wanted to say it outloud, get it out of my head.

Monkey and Blain

Blain: Does it help?

Monkey: eh....Cats on the Internet.......a little better now.... MAGIC BANANAS!...a little better. Dogs in cars.....HA HA HA HA HA HA HA.....ok, now im better.

Blain: Dogs in cars make me smile too.

Monkey: They are FLYING! Steaksauce!

Monkey: Hey Blain, Do you want to know what I think?

Blain: What's up monkey?

Monkey: Well I think that .

Blain: WHOA! Holy Crap! That is the most disturbing and filthy and terrifying thing I have ever heard. You should probably keep that to yourself. We live in America, but I don't think that should be said out loud. Again.

Monkey: Crap. So, this will stay between you and me?

Blain: Indeed.

Aliens/Facebook/TV

Monkey: Why do all the experts and scientists on 'Ancient Aliens' look high?

Blain: Because they are probably high.

Monkey: Sounds accurate. Some aliens are killed by salt.

Blain: Most likely.

Monkey: Earth is covered with salt.

Blain: we are safe!

Monkey: Blain, why do people think aliens are more advanced than humans?

Blain: What are you talking about?

Monkey: All the TV shows about aliens stating how more advanced the aliens would be.

Blain: First, you need to stop watching alien shows on TV. Second, I think the alien experts, for the most part, don't believe in God. They know something is smarter than humans, but don't believe it could be God, so it must be aliens.

Monkey: Sounds crazy when you say it that way.

Blain: I think if there are aliens, they are just as messed up as humans. If they ever came to Earth it would be by accident or a wrong turn...like when Columbus discovered 'India'.

Monkey and Blain

Monkey: Blain, I have another beef.

Blain: Ok, vent away monkey.

Monkey: Why do people take so many photos of themselves in bathrooms? It's just weird.

Blain: Feel better?

Monkey: A little. We should take a bunch of photos of use making duckfaces in the bathroom.

Blain: Um, no.

Monkey: Come on, everyone is doing it.

Blain: Not everyone.

Monkey: DO IT DO IT DO IT DO IT.

Blain: Still not happening.

Monkey: Wuss.

Blain: Yep.

Monkey: No argument?

Blain: Nope.

Monkey: Wait up! I found a photo of you in the bathroom!

Blain: Yeah?

Monkey: You were shaving.

Blain: I shave in the bathroom.

Monkey: Why the photo?

Blain: I think I was making fun, or trying different shaving styles....I have no idea.

Monkey: Maybe people were in the bathroom, just dropped a huge poop and thought 'hey, i bet im looking good after dumping off that huge smelly loaf, I better snap a photo'.

Blain: Probably not.

Monkey: Dare to dream.

Monkey: Hey Blain?

Blain: yes monkey?

Monkey: What is 'Fortnite'?

Blain: It is 2 weeks.

Monkey: What?

Blain: What?

Monkey: I think it is a game.

Blain: If you knew, why did you ask? Why is there a game about 2 weeks?

Monkey: You like those games.

Blain: It is called fortnight?

Monkey: Yep.

Blain: Never heard of it.

Monkey: You said it was 14 days.

Monkey and Blain

Blain: Yes, a fortnight is 14 days.

Monkey: What?

Blain: What?

Monkey: So, im watching TV....

Blain: Big surprise.

Monkey: Wiseassery....anyway, watching TV, I saw a commercial for osteoporosis, anyhow, this actress steps out onto a stage, raises her hands to applause, then continues the commercial.

Blain: Ok?

Monkey: I was thinking how weird it would be to receive applause wherever you went.

Blain: So you wouldn't want to be famous?

Monkey: No way! Too awkward. Everywhere you went, wanting your attention, snapping photos. Too much.

Blain: Me either. I would love to be totally off grid, but the whole job thing. I wouldn't mind being wealthy, but not known.

Monkey: Me too....except I have no job, no ssn, don't pay taxes.....wait, I AM unknown!

Blain: Exactly, stay unknown.

Monkey: In fact, I don't even have a name....

Blain: Not again, you are not getting a name. Naming you would confirm my mental state.

Monkey: cause you are perfectly sane now, right?

Blain: Exactly.

Monkey: Steak..

Blain: ..Sauce.

Monkey: No Facebook, I CANT tell you what is on my mind. It freaks people out. Everything is great, everyone is great.... blah blah blah and all that. Maybe if we all began to be real then we would know how someone is actually doing.

Blain: I concur.

Monkey: Just living in a daydream, unreality, not talking about anything, don't start stuff, won't be stuff, carry on sheepy, carry on.

Blain: Truth.

Monkey: Blain, I posted something onto your Facebook.

Blain: Great. What was it?

Monkey: Collecting donations.

Blain: For what?

Monkey: Ok, selling something.

Blain: Which is it?

Monkey and Blain

Monkey: I posted that I would tell them the meaning of life for $1.00 per person, $10.00 per group, or release it to the world for $1,000,000,000.

Blain: Another scam?

Monkey: Nah, I do know the meaning of life.

Blain: What is it?

Monkey: Pay up.

Blain: Nope.

Monkey: Live in wonder then.

Blain: Fine with me.

Monkey: Survival shows are awesome! I know how to get water from a banana tree.

Blain: Great. We don't have banana trees in Iowa though.

Monkey: You sure?

Blain: I've seen most of Iowa, haven't seen 1 banana tree.

Monkey: Oh well. If I hunt a deer with a spear, do I need a hunting license?

Blain: Probably not, you are imaginary.

Monkey: Would you need a license?

Blain: I don't plan on deer hunting with a spear.

Monkey: Fine. I know how to properly skin a rabbit and

make a pig sticker trap.

Blain: Useful.

Monkey: I can make my own soap too. I don't want to, but I am able to.

Blain: One day I may need to call on your skills.

Monkey: Deal!

Monkey: I'm sexy and I know it...wiggle wiggle wiggle wiggle wiggle wiggle wiggle.

Blain: ....

Monkey: Exactly.

Monkey: Can I still say 'steaksauce'?

Blain: Yeah, why?

Monkey: It is from a TV show.

Blain: And?

Monkey: What if they sued?

Blain: Good luck with that, sue an imaginary monkey.

Monkey: Good point.

Monkey: Did I miss the super football game thing?

Blain: By almost a full month.

Monkey: Did the Cubs win it again?

Blain: Yep.

Monkey: GOOOOOO CUBS!

Blain: Steaksauce.

Monkey: We should start a TV show.

Blain: Why?

Monkey: Judge Judy will make 180 million in 4 years.

Blain: WOW.

Monkey: So we could do some show, give away most of the money. If my math is correct, using Judge Judy money, it is like 45 million per year. Keep like 10%.

Blain: Yes. Who would need more than 4.5 million per year?

Monkey: Not me.

Blain: No me either.

Monkey: Make it happen.

Blain: We need an idea first.

Monkey: Working on it.

Monkey: Watched about 5 mins of the people in a house TV show.

Blain: What did you think?

Monkey: Bunch of trash. Guys are douches and gals are whiney.

Blain: A solid critique.

Monkey: A solid D. Honey boo and everyone on that show need a slap too.

Blain: Won't last.

Monkey: We will see.

Monkey: What sucks.....sorry....'sips' is when famous people use their names to hock other products and such.

Blain: Like spokespeople?

Monkey: No, that isn't too terrible. I mean like a MMA fighter selling their photos, or an actress making makeup, or even like staying around so long that you are just making money from your name....like the 29th reunion tour of some band that was great but now just cashing in.

Blain: Understandable. What about it makes you so upset?

Monkey: Not sure....maybe it is people who actually buy the stuff just due to it being from a famous person.

Blain: Sounds fair.

Monkey: Like how Servant Guitars never went anywhere, or how not many people will ever see the book.

Blain: Stepping on the little people and startups!

Monkey and Blain

Monkey: Yeah.

Blain: Yeah. Makes you wanna spit.

Monkey: And cuss.

Blain: Feel better?

Monkey: no.

Blain: These survival shows are pretty good.

Monkey: I'm gonna make a bow and arrow.

Blain: Ok, go for it.

Monkey: Can I shoot birds in the backyard?

Blain: Only if you are gonna eat them.

Monkey: Not unless I had to.

Blain: If you shoot it, you have to eat it.

Monkey: Eh. Can I make traps?

Blain: For what?

Monkey: Squirrels, rabbits....goats.

Blain: Goats?

Monkey: None in Iowa?

Blain: Not in the backyard.

Monkey: Ok, maybe no goats.

Blain: Anyhow, the answer is still no, no traps.

Monkey: You 'sip'.

Blain: I know what you are really saying.

Monkey: Good.

Blain: Go get to shaving wood. Bow won't make itself.

Monkey: Oh, right. Making a bow!

Monkey: Blain, remember the TV show I created?

Blain: 'Chasing Unicorns with Monkey'?

Monkey: Yep, it got cancelled.

Blain: That is terrible. Why did it get cancelled?

Monkey: So we were filming last week at ██████ forest. We actually found a unicorn.

Blain: That is great! But why did the show get cancelled? It didn't have to be a series, it could have been a breaking news or something.

Monkey: Let me finish. We filmed the unicorn for about 30 minutes, watched it eat, solid proof of a unicorn. Then out of nowhere bigfoot came out and attacked the unicorn. Got it all on film.

Blain: A Unicorn AND bigfoot?

Monkey: Yep, took an hour for bigfoot to eat the unicorn. Filmed it all.

Blain: But why was the show cancelled? This sounds like a gold mine!

Monkey: Then aliens came down and abducted bigfoot. All on tape.

Blain: HOLY CRAP! 3 for 3 proofs!

Monkey: Yep, then, these guys in military uniforms arrived and seized the tapes. We had to sign a NDA.

Blain: They took the film, so no proof.

Monkey: Right. I would sound insane to tell the story.

Blain: Pretty sneaky.

Monkey: It will be ok. I just wanted to have a TV show.

Blain: Dream big monkey!

Monkey: One day maybe.

Monkey: I'm going to comment on Facebook posts.

Blain: No swearing.

Monkey: I won't, just gonna comment 'Right On!' to everyone i read.

Blain: What if they are negative?

Monkey: 'Right on!'

Blain: I think this is terrific plan.

Monkey: YES!

Monkey: I'm pretty sure God doesn't care if I 'share this post' 10 times.

Blain: What are you talking about?

Monkey: Facebook, share this image of Jesus and be blessed crap.

Blain: Just wishful thinking, not faith.

Monkey: Bunch of crap it is.

Blain: Yep.

Monkey: Believe and receive my foot! I've wanted wings and a billion dollars for years.

Blain: I don't see any wings, and I know you don't have a billion dollars.

Monkey: True and true.

Monkey: Well, lemme tell ya a story 'bout a man named Blain, spent all his days just living in his brain. Then one day got sick of people's poop, and moved on out to the wilderness and was eaten by a bear....Chewy....Chewy and crunchy he was....

Blain: Beverly Hillbillies?

Monkey: Couldn't think of anything that rhymes with poop....but serious, don't move to the woods, you will die.

Blain: Don't know if we don't try.

Monkey: Bear poop he is...smelly smelly pie.

Blain: Whatever.

Monkey: Fine, but I will run when the bear eats you.

Blain: I'm willing to risk it.

Monkey: Get to packing.

Monkey: I was flipping channels.

Blain: Find anything good?

Monkey: Saw a product called 'Light Angel' or 'Angel Light'... it will light up everytime a human, pet or automobile passes by.

Blain: And?

Monkey: Zero mention of aliens or ghosts or monsters.

Blain: Pretty lame.

Monkey: Yep, I want a light that shows the monsters too!

Blain: So basically, this light was just another motion sensor light?

Monkey: Yep, I think I will pass.

Blain: Good call.

Monkey: Diddily dee diddily poop diddily bebop yeo dang a ling a do day.

Monkey: Blain Blain Blain, guess what tooooooodays is?

Blain: October?

Monkey: Nope, its SEXXXXXXXY DAYYYYY!

Blain: WHAT?!?!

Monkey: Why is it funny when the camel says it?

Blain: OH, probably cause it is called 'hump day' and does NOT mean what you think it does.

Monkey: That explains a lot…..so, Blain….guess what toooooday is?

Blain: Im sticking with October.

Monkey: Woot Woot YEEEAAAH….wait, you were supposed to say 'hump day'.

Blain: It may actually be Thursday.

Monkey: Why don't we know what day it is?

Blain: Work.

Monkey: Sucks to be you, slave to the Man, I'm gonna eat flapjacks.

Monkey: I watched a program called "Manson'.

Blain: Why?

Monkey: Wanted to see what it was about.

Blain: Charles Manson?

Monkey: Yep, you heard of him?

Monkey and Blain

Blain: Yep. What did you learn.

Monkey: Want to know what you and Charles Manson have in common?

Blain: Not really.

Monkey: You are both white males.

Blain: That's it?

Monkey: That's it.

Monkey: Blain, you know a bunch of bi-polar people on Facebook.

Blain: What?

Monkey: Check these out....I'm good, life is hard. I'm good.....people stink. I'm good, I love everyone....I can't stand people.

Blain: Ah ha.

Monkey: Consistency people, consistency.

Blain: What Monkey said.

Monkey: Want to know what I'm thinking?

Blain: Nope.

Monkey: Sissy. Bunch of bubble wrapped pansies.

Blain: Who?

Monkey: You know.

Blain: I haven't the foggiest.

Monkey: All of them.

Blain: Oky Doky.

Monkey: Steak sauce! Blain still 'sips'.

Monkey: Hey Blain, can we contact the Ghost hunter TV people?

Blain: Why?

Monkey: I have a great idea.

Blain: What is that?

Monkey: We tell them the house is haunted, but before they come we set up a bunch of things to screw with them.

Blain: This sounds interesting.

Monkey: Hide inside the house and make noises and rig stuff up to move around, random electric pulses.

Blain: That would be fun, but what if we were caught?

Monkey: But, what if they didn't figure it out, and it got aired. They would look like a bunch of jackasses.....we could contact the bigfoot people too!

Blain: Now you are talking! Let's do both!

Monkey: You make the calls, I will rig the house.

Blain: Deal.

Monkey: There is a show called 'keeping up with the kardashians?'

Blain: Yep.

Monkey: Dear Lord Jesus, take me now.

Blain: Not a fan?

Monkey: I dont give 2 poops what they are doing.

Blain: This would be a much funnier conversation in the future.

Monkey: Why is that?

Blain: Bruce becomes Kaitlyn.

Monkey: WHAT?!!?!?

Monkey: Blain, I've been watching competition survival shows. There are a lot of them.

Blain: True.

Monkey: I think I would kick butt on these shows.

Blain: Yeah? Why is that?

Monkey: Cause I'm a monkey.

Blain: A monkey that has never lived in the wild.

Monkey: True, but it can't be that hard.

Blain: Go try to make a fire out back.

Monkey: Challenge accepted!

5 minutes later

Monkey: This is hard.

Blain: Yep, harder than it looks, isn't it?

Monkey: Well, I would bring a flint stick. Problem solved.

Blain: Then there is the matter of eating and shelter.

Monkey: Easy and easy, I would eat the other competitors and use their skin for a hut.

Blain: Gross!

Monkey: Just kidding. I don't think I want to play anymore.

Blain: Probably for the best.

Monkey: What about a game show, I would be good at that.

Blain: Well, you are intelligent, but I don't think TV is ready for you. Cable maybe, but not network.

Monkey: Yeah.

Blain: Maybe exposure from the book will get you on TV.

Monkey: Shameless.

Blain: A little.

Monkey: Grand master of promoting.

Blain: Indeed.

Monkey: What does cocaine do for you that no one else does?

Monkey and Blain

Blain: What?

Monkey: Radio commercial...oh, they said 'club cadet'

Blain: I wouldn't think they said cocaine.

Monkey: I thought maybe Kansas lost its mind.

Blain: Or the pet food commercial.

Monkey: HAHAHAHA, 'does your dog stink, scratch or shit like crazy?'

Blain: Yeah, that one.

Monkey: Poopin dogs....you didn't censor my use of 'shit'.

Blain: Giving you a little space. Don't abuse it.

Monkey: Awesome! *BLEEP BLEEP BLEEP BLEEP*.

Blain: 13 seconds, a new record. And back to censoring you.

Monkey: *BLEEP*

Monkey: Hey Blain?

Blain: Yes monkey?

Monkey: I think they really aren't preparing or zombies.

Blain: Sounds like they aren't.

Monkey: But what if the zombies get us?

Blain: They won't Monkey.

Monkey: Why not?

Blain: We will be taxed to death first.

Monkey: Like thumb tacks?

Blain: No, Taxes, like paying money to live in this country, help afford things in the government.

Monkey: That sounds illegal.

Blain: Kinda, but they use the money to do things like re-pave the roads.

Monkey: HA HA HA HA HA HA HA HA, Repave the roads? When are they gonna start?

Blain: They do it constantly.

Monkey: Have you driven on the roads? They are terrible!

Blain: Yes true, but we pay taxes to help us and others out.

Monkey: That's crap, they aren't doing anything with the tax money.

Blain: Ok, Probably not, but what do we do?

Monkey: Stop paying taxes.

Blain: That is illegal.

Monkey: Illegal Schmlegal...fine give me a couple days, ill figure something out. So we decided we don't need to worry about zombies?

Blain: Yes Monkey, no worrying about zombies.

Monkey: Ok, you da boss. Give me a few days, I will figure out what we can do about taxes.

Monkey and Blain

Monkey: Hey Blain, what is the first rule of fight club?

Blain: I can't tell you.

Monkey: Come on. You can tell me...what is the first rule of fight club?

Blain: Well the first rule of fight club is...

SMACK

Blain: OWWWW! What the hell monkey?

Monkey: We don't talk about it. It was a test, you failed.

Blain: Don't hit me monkey.

Monkey: Rules are rules, don't be a pansy.

Blain: Ok....i will repay.

Monkey: Still mad?

Blain: Nope. I was just thinking. What is the first rule of fight club?

Monkey: It's...

SMACK

Monkey: OWWWWW!

Blain: Now we are even.

Monkey: Well played.

Blain: Ice cream?

Monkey and Blain Diebolt

Monkey: Yes please.

Monkey: So.

Blain: Yeah?

Monkey: Yep.

Blain: And?

Monkey: That's it.

Blain: You sure?

Monkey: .....Steaksauce.

Blain: Thought so.

MONKEY ON RELIGION AND GOD

Monkey: So there is this catchy tune about the drive thru difference.

Blain: Yep, paying it forward.

Monkey: I like helping people too, but paying it forward in a drive thru is nuts.

Blain: How so?

Monkey: What about the people who aren't in the drive thru?

Blain: Good point.

Monkey: Making Christianity a joke, a game, entertainment.

Blain: Yep, love God, love people.

Monkey: Saved by Grace.

Blain: Exactly.

Monkey: Wait, the pope retired? Is that allowed?

Blain: Seems so.

Monkey: So what now? Just no pope?

Blain: Not sure, it has only happened 2 times in the last 600 years.

Monkey: Were you there for the 1st one? Can I be pope?

Blain: WIseass. No and no.

Monkey: Cause I'm not a Catholic?

Blain: Sure, let's go with that.

Monkey: Ok, I fox news'd it. Pope retired, he is tired.

Blain: Ok, so what happens?

Monkey: I Googled the next pope. Some dude named Malachy predicted in 1100 AD-ish, that there would only be 112 popes, and that the next pope is the LAST pope. POPECOPLYPSE!

Blain: That is not a thing.

Monkey: Is now.

Monkey: Blain, I know Jesus' middle name.

Blain: Jesus? As in The Lord Jesus?

Monkey: Yep, I know His middle name.

Blain: Ok, what is it?

Monkey: Marion.

Blain: Marion? Who told you that?

Monkey: Homeless guy downtown, he said 'JESUS MARION JOSEPH, A TALKING MONKEY!' Then he ran away. What time is it by the way, the guy never said.

Blain: 12:15....a few things we need to go over. #1 Don't go downtown by yourself anymore, it freaks people out. #2, it is a saying. The guy said "Jesus, Mary and Joseph'. We dont know Jesus's middle name.

Monkey: So it isn't Marion? I suppose God's name isnt Andy either?

Blain: Old joke, a good one, an old one, but a good one. No more downtown by yourself.

Monkey: I promise.

Blain: Good monkey.

Blain's health and doctor appointments

Blain was diagnosed with kidney problems and microscopic hematuria in 2012

Blain: You've been quiet all week, feeling ok?

Monkey: Yeah, im ok.

Blain: You sound a little bummed. Is everything ok?

Monkey: I was thinking that when you die, I die right?

Blain: yes. I believe that is true. Does that frighten you?

Monkey: No. Just kinda bums me out.

Blain: Is it because I went to the doctor again? No news is good news.

Monkey: What if they give you bad news?

Blain: Then we deal with it when it comes. Dont worry about it. Want to know the secret of immortality?

Monkey: Yes. What is it?

Blain: Tell your story. You will live forever.

Monkey: That is pretty kickass.

Blain: Read it in a book.

Monkey: Neat!

Blain: What is your favorite part of today?

Monkey: COWS! MOOOOOOOOOOOOOOOOOOOO!

Blain: Yes, the cows. Enjoy today, don't worry about future things.

Monkey: MOOOOOOOOOOOOOOOO! That one looked!

Blain: I scheduled time off for the doctor appointment.

Monkey: What is it for?

Blain: Kidney doctor.

Monkey: You dying?

Blain: Nope, they found blood in my urine.

Monkey: You pee blood?

Blain: It is microscopic.

Monkey: How'd they find out?

Blain: Microscopes I assume.

Monkey: Why were they looking?

Blain: No idea.

Monkey: That was awkward.

Blain: Well she asked.

Monkey: Didn't have to use the flashy thing on her though.

Blain: She couldn't handle the truth, it had to be done.

Monkey: HA HA HA HA HA, she couldn't find your pulse,

said you were dead.

Blain: Don't make me use the flasher on you too.

Monkey: Right. Nevermind.

Blain: Hey monkey?

Monkey: What up Bro-izzle?

Blain: What?...nevermind. I'm cold monkey.

Monkey: Probably the blood loss.

Blain: I'm bleeding?

Monkey: Don't freak out nancy, the peeing thing.

Blain: I'm not peeing THAT much blood.

Monkey: My second guess….you are a sissy.

Blain: And I'm kinda bored.

Monkey: And? What would you like me to do about it? Dance?

Blain: Nah, just saying.

Monkey: Know what you gotta do?

Blain: I don't 'gotta' do nothing except pay taxes and die.

Monkey: We aren't immortal?

Blain: Possibly, but not definitely. Eternal soul, yes.

Monkey: So what is the plan?

Blain: Watch TV then try to sleep, make calls tomorrow I guess.

Monkey: Just chillaxin tonight?

Blain: Yep.

Monkey: Steaaaaaaaaaaaaaak Sauuuuuuuuuuuce!

Blain: Sure.

Monkey: Pre-diabetic?

Blain: That is what they said.

Monkey: Isn't everyone who doesn't have diabetes already, pre-diabetic?

Blain: That was my thought too.

Monkey: Like being alive is pre-dead, and being awake is pre-sleeping.

Blain: Both true.

Monkey: No more doctors.

Blain: Agreed.

Monkey: Just to clear things up....there is NO SUCH THING as an increased risk of death. At birth, your risk of death is 100%, no matter what you do between birth and the end... which is death...your 'risk' of death is 100%. Premature death is an actual thing, but only God knows when you will die. That is all.

Blain: Feel better?

Monkey: A little. Can i rant about gas pumps in winter?

Blain: Go for it, I'm here for you.

Monkey: In order to purchase gas, I need to select credit or debit, choose a pump, enter the pin, yes for receipt, no for car wash, fuel saver card or no, wait for the inside approval. I JUST WANT THE *BLEEP*ING GAS! It is cold, it is windy, just give me the gas and let me leave!

Blain: Ok, now are you better?

Monkey: Magic bananas.

Monkey: Blain, I was looking at your calendar.

Blain: And?

Monkey: You have 3 doctor appointments this week.

Blain: Yeah?

Monkey: What for?

Blain: Blood drawn, nephrologist and urologist.

Monkey: What the flying poop is a nephrologist?

Blain: Kidney doctor.

Monkey: And a Urologist?

Blain: Urinary tract doctor.

Monkey: something wrong with your ding dong?

Blain: That is the 'peeing doctor'.

Monkey: Oh right, the blood thing. Are you gonna die?

Blain: We are all gonna die monkey.

Monkey: I mean cause of the bleeding.

Blain: I don't think so, but that is why I go to the doctors.

Monkey: Hasn't this been going on for a while?

Blain: Yes, same thing since 2012.

Monkey: You aren't dead yet.

Blain: Right.

Monkey: How do you feel?

Blain: I feel the same as I always have.

Monkey: Old and grouchy?

Blain: Exactly.

2015ish

Monkey: Hey Blain, did you know nicotine and caffeine are pesticides?

Blain: I actually did know that.

Monkey: So why do you use them?

Blain: Glad you asked, let me tell you my feelings on this. I think it is important to ingest toxins on a regular basis. But be careful with them, too much and you are dead, too little

Monkey and Blain

and it is pointless. The idea is to consume enough toxins in order to build up an immunity to toxins and not over do it to death.

Monkey: What?

Blain: Think about it, we are poisoning everything around us. By taking in some toxins daily, I am building up my immunity to toxins and when all our filtering things stop and toxins get out of hand worldwide, i will be immune to the pollution.

Monkey: WHAT?!? THAT IS INSANE!

Blain: I'm a science experiment, determining if a person can live primarily off cigarettes and diet soda.

Monkey: I think you are making *BLEEP* up.

Blain: Ok, ok, we use them as stimulants because we are all overworked, rushed and don't get enough rest.

Monkey: THAT sounds like the truth.

Blain: You will be a truth bringer Monkey. Be brave, be fierce.

Monkey: Darn tootin! NEW MONKEY REVOLUTION COMING!

Blain: 19 days.

Monkey: Screw you.

Blain: What?

Monkey: Still not lovin it, no ba da ba ba ba.

Blain: Getting better though.

Monkey: Lets get cigars.

Blain: Lets see how we do after 21 days.

Monkey: Fine.

Blain: You sure?

Monkey: Maybe I need a Snickers.

Blain: You do get a little grumpy when you are hungry.

Monkey: Steaksauce.

Monkey: Why are people staring?

Blain: You told them we may have parasites.

Monkey: They asked how I was doing.

Blain: Not what they meant.

Monkey: It may be true.

Blain: Not a good response as church greeter.

Monkey: IT MAY BE TRUE!

Blain: They want you to respond 'I'm good, how are you?'.

Monkey: Lame. Don't ask if you don't mean it.

Blain: Yep.

Monkey and Blain

Monkey: Blain, you should quit smoking.

Blain: I know this.

Monkey: Just dont use the prescriptions to stop.

Blain: Why is that?

Monkey: The warnings on those drugs include suicidal thoughts and actions, change in mood, nausea....

Blain: Good point, while I'm detoxing and feeling like crap, going through withdrawals and changing habits and such, please add more stress and symptoms to the slice of hell.

Monkey: Yeah, screw that, but you should quit.

Blain: One day I will. I've tried before, will try again.

Monkey: I remember, every second was like hell.

Blain: Yep, and I need to want to quit.

Monkey: Yeah, maybe wait til then. We don't need to tilt the cart at this time.

Blain: Yeah.

Monkey: Yeah.

Blain: Did I take my meds?

Monkey: How would I know?

Blain: You are always here.

Monkey: We share a brain. If you can't remember, how can i?

Blain: Good point.

Monkey: So, did you take your meds?

Blain: I'm going with 'probably'.

Monkey: What happens when you miss them?

Blain: I explode.

Monkey: WHAT?!?!?

Blain: I'm joking Monkey. Nothing actually happens. I would have to miss for weeks.

Monkey: AH, then *BLEEP* it.

Blain: Language.

Monkey: Blain, your doctor's office called and asked when your last diabetic eye exam was.

Blain: What did you tell them?

Monkey: I told them to cram it in their....

Blain: Please tell me you didn't.

Monkey: No, I politely told them that you don't have diabetes.

Blain: What did they say to that?

Monkey: That they wanted to talk to you.

Blain: Are they still on the phone?

Monkey: Nope. I hung up. What kind of doctor, that has you medical records, doesn't know if you have diabetes or not?

Blain: Good point.

Blain: Good news, im not diabetic and I'm allowed to grow a beard.

Monkey: That isn't what he said.

Blain: Shut up Monkey.

Monkey: Come on, say it.

Blain: No.

Monkey: Either you admit it or I will repeat it all day long.

Blain: Fine. He said I was allowed to grow a beard if I could grow a beard.

Monkey: HAHAHAHA, Blain hasn't hit puberty yet.....39 years old!

Blain: Bite me Monkey.......OUCH!

Monkey: You told me to.

Blain: It is a figure of speech.

Monkey: I really don't like figures of speech. Sorry babyface.

Blain: Watch it!

Monkey: Steaksauce.

Monkey: It is probably not even true.

Monkey and Blain Diebolt

Blain: IF it was true, that what you eat, exercise and health living and such, I would have died years ago.

Monkey: Zombie Blain!

Blain: The nurse did say walking corpse syndrome.

Monkey: I Googled it, that isn't what it means.

Blain: Wonder if she knew.

Monkey: My guess? No. stop going to doctors.

Blain: Steaksauce.

Monkey: Blain, I don't like what the doctor said.

Blain: I honestly wasn't listening.

Monkey: I think it was pow pow pow pow pow dangalangadingdong.

Blain: I think that is what the fox said.

Monkey: Oh, that's right, the doctor said, CAW CAW CAW.

Blain: That is what a crow says.

Monkey: So what did the doctor say?

Blain: Don't know, wasn't listening. Come back in 6 months, get your blood drawn,

Monkey: Ah, rinse and repeat.

Blain: Exactly.

Blain: Good thing we got here early.

Monkey: Doctor is late = no problem, patient late = counts as a missed appointment, still charged even if no actual treatment.

Blain: Bet they tell me that I am still alive.

Monkey: Would be a better story if they told you that you died.

Blain: True. And waiting waiting waiting. Good thing I don't work on wednesdays.

Monkey: What? I thought you did work on weekdays.

Blain: Sarcasm Monkey.

Monkey: I can never tell with you.

Blain: Lots of practice.

Monkey: Well done.

In 2019, Blain no longer has to go to the Nephrologist.

Monkey: THAT IS FANTASTIC!

Blain: Indeed. No more kidney doctor.

Monkey: Did they say why?

Blain: They can't prove that my kidneys are failing, and no longer consider me in any risk or danger. Depending on what you believe, either God healed me, or the consistent diet of cigarettes and Diet Dew did.

Monkey: And the last 7 years of treatment?

Blain: No explanation.

Monkey: Lame. Think it was a money making scam?

Blain: Possibly, but no more. I am free!

Monkey: That is good news. Still pee blood?

Blain: Yep, but it is still microscopic, and after 7 years and numerous tests, they don't know why.

Monkey: 'practicing medicine' not 'performing medicine'.

Blain: Yep. Still free!

Monkey: Yeah, let's go eat candy!

Blain: Deal.

And here ends the select collection of conversations between Monkey and Blain. All of these conversations actually took place between November 2012 and November 2019. If you would like to be part of the upcoming book 'Ask Monkey Anything', please go to the Facebook page *'Monkey and Blain'* and submit your question. Not all questions will be included so be unique in what you would like Monkey to answer. Thank you for reading, and be a doer in life. Steaksauce.

Monkey and Blain live at Danland in Cedar Rapids IA.
Connect with them on Facebook; @Monkey and Blain

CPSIA information can be obtained
at www.ICGtesting.com
Printed in the USA
LVHW010154030320
648723LV00002B/503